THE LOVE OF MARY

STEVE SHELLEY

Copyright © 2021 by Steve Shelley and Alanna Rusnak Publishing

This book is a work of fiction inspired by the Biblical narrative.

All rights reserved. This book or any portion thereof may not be reproduced or used in any manner whatsoever without the express written permission of the publisher except for the use of brief quotations in a book review or scholarly journal.

www.theloveofmary.com

First Printing: 2021
ALANNA RUSNAK PUBLISHING
ISBN: 978-1-990336-10-2

Alanna Rusnak Publishing
282906 Normanby/Bentinck Townline
Durham, Ontario, Canada, N0G 1R0

www.alannarusnakpublishing.com

Cover art by Amos Shelley
amosshelley.com

To those who love the mystery of Christmas

and the stories it inspires.

THE LOVE OF MARY

STEVE SHELLEY

2021

Chapter One
The Wood Shop

The shop wasn't much to look at, just a lean-to structure built on the back of a stone house, typical for the working classes in Nazareth. Stones along the top of the wall enclosing the flat roof of the house were removed to allow timbers to be inserted. These sloped down to a low wall built of poles dug into the ground. Rough tent cloth stretched over the roof timbers, keeping out the sun and the occasional rain.

The scent of wood permeated the shop air. Fragrant cedars from Lebanon mixed with pungent sycamores from the Jordan Valley, heady oaks from the slopes of Mt. Tabor, and bitter figs from Samaria. Each end of the shop housed pairs of doors wide enough to span the entire wall. During the day these doors were flung open to enlarge the work space.

Joseph laboured in the open air of the shop, the sun hot on his back. He straddled a narrow beam, his knees clamping a block of fir he was shaping into a roof bracket. As he guided the chisel into the wood with deliberate strokes of the mallet, shavings of wood and sawdust glued to the sweat of his forearm.

"I would have made a good patriarch," he mused aloud to himself. "Jacob disguised himself by covering his arms with sheep wool to deceive his father into thinking he was his hairy brother Esau. I could do the same trick with wood shavings."

As he spoke, he shifted the position of the beam so he could look beyond the shop to the town below. The shop sat at the end of a street that gave way to the hill behind it to the south. Joseph's father had worked as a carpenter with his cousins in this same spot. They had been a good team, and many of the homes Joseph gazed upon as he worked were ones for which his father had built the roof beams, the window frames, and the doors.

Joseph's mother passed when he was only a year old, and so he was the only child of his father. It was at one of those homes—Joseph tried not to remember which one—that the accident happened. His father had been fitting a roof beam along the top of the wall when the stonework gave way. As he lost his balance and fell to the ground, the beam he was working on crashed down on top of him, leaving Joseph to face the world as an orphan.

All of Joseph's father's plans were crushed out of him and he didn't have a chance to do the things most fathers did. No chance to apprentice Joseph, then only nine. No chance to tell Joseph one more time how much he loved him. No chance to complete all the things he wanted to finish in their own home. No chance to leave Joseph with his own shop and tools to build a business.

That is how Joseph came to labour at the shop of his father's cousin Obadiah. When he completed his schooling at the age of twelve and was not chosen as one of the brightest to continue, Joseph began to apprentice as a carpenter. Obadiah would not let him work on an actual home site; instead, Joseph toiled in the shop, making all the wooden components that go into the building of a stone house: doors, thresholds, windowsills, cornices, brackets, and the cursed roof beams.

But Joseph had plans of his own. As often as he could he practised building furniture. Using the skill he developed building doors, he constructed tables that could be widened for feasts by the simple insertion of an extra board. He was working on a bench that had sides to keep small children from sliding off.

He had improved the type of windowsills that had been in use for decades by sloping the top edge so rain, when it did come, would drip only outside the wall. He built shutters for windows that, when closed, would keep out most of the rain and dust on windy days. His latest project was a lamp stand with a base of stones that even the most rambunctious child could not knock over.

He longed to build a home in the hills surrounding Nazareth. The hills were scattered with flowers and flowering shrubs all year round, setting a foundation for the spectacular scenery beyond. On a good day you could see the white snow of Mt. Tabor to the north, the aqua green of the Sea of Galilee to the east, and all the variety of hills and rocky outcrops in between. But the real reason Joseph wanted to have a home in the hills was a reason he never shared with anyone. He wanted to plant trees, nurture them, and eventually harvest them to use as raw material for building his furniture.

Trees in Galilee were not plentiful. Centuries of harvesting by his ancestors had seen to that. And the hot, arid climate did not allow trees of any substance to grow without aid. Just as a farmer would nourish an olive grove and harvest its fruit, so too would he husband his own crop of trees, growing exactly the species he needed. While the trees were still young and supple, he would use rocks and ropes to coax them to grow into the curves he wanted. He would be able to harvest them at the peak of their strength and beauty. With this kind of raw material Joseph could build the finest furniture in Nazareth, maybe even fine enough to be used in the synagogue.

The Nazareth synagogue was simple, resembling the working class of the people it served. The stand from which the scrolls were read each Sabbath was adequate, but it would look like an animal's feed trough compared to the stand he would build. Its feet would be weighted with five stones fitted into the base to symbolize the Torah. Its pedestal would be carved to resemble an ephod, complete with a carving of the Urim and Thummin. The top would have rolled edges to look like an open scroll, complete with a tassel. Rubbed with oil from his own olive trees, Joseph's stand would gleam in the dullest light. Such beauty of form and function would even be at home at the temple in Jerusalem.

Such were the dreams that Joseph nurtured as he laboured in the sun on the common building components for Obadiah. Occasionally, he would gaze down the streets to the hills beyond, lost in thoughts of the beautiful furniture he would one day create.

There was another reason that he wished to build a home in the hills above Nazareth, a reason that he almost hesitated to share with himself. As he gazed down the streets he could see the rooftop that housed that reason...Mary.

Joseph's childhood friend Caleb lived in one of the narrow homes in the lower streets of Nazareth. Caleb's parents were much older than Joseph's, so much of their time as children was spent at Caleb's house, helping him finish household chores before they could go into the streets to play. They spent long evenings together there, teasing each other and everyone else, especially Caleb's younger sister Mary.

Although he had known her all his life, Joseph had given Mary no special notice. As they grew older, Joseph and Caleb would venture beyond town to explore the hills, and often Mary would tag along.

Caleb and Mary's cousins were in the priesthood so their family was faithful to journey to Jerusalem every year for the Passover. While there, four years earlier, Mary's father took ill. Even the best medicine and care in Jerusalem was not enough. He never made it back to Nazareth alive. Within a year, Mary's mother took to her bed of a broken heart and failing health and she died as well.

At her mother's funeral, Joseph saw Mary as if for the first time. No longer the little girl he teased in the dusty streets of Nazareth, she had become a young lady, her dark eyes shining with strength in the midst of her sorrow. Gleaming hair framed a face that was youthful yet mature, and she moved with confidence during that time despite the confusion.

The days of mourning turned into months of caring for her parent's affairs and keeping the home functioning for Caleb. Joseph visited as often as he could, finding reasons to talk to her. Their friendship blossomed as they shared the sorrow of a father snatched from them in their youth.

The talks progressed into long walks into the hills. Most of her family came from the hill country of Judea and she had visited them often during their annual treks to the feasts in Jerusalem. She loved the solitude of the country, and the views that greeted her at the crest of each rise of land. She admired the varieties of flowers, shrubs, and vegetables that could be grown. Joseph shared his dream of a home in the hills and soon it was no longer his dream but theirs.

Yet for all the time they had spent together in the past years, Joseph was still hesitant. He hadn't saved up enough money to build them a home. All he had saved so far was only enough to buy the plot of land, and even that he was reluctant to spend. He couldn't bring Mary to live at Obadiah's house, and there was no way to turn the shop into a home. They could move into Caleb's house, but Caleb was now a merchant and considering selling the house to move down to Jerusalem. Besides, settling for a house in town would mean giving up their dream of living in the hills. Joseph and Mary wanted their children to be able to run through the flowers in the fields, not through the dusty streets of town.

Mary was now of marriageable age and if he didn't make his intention public, he risked losing her to another. If he could work harder and longer for just one more year, he might be in a position to buy the land and begin to build their home. His gaze left the street and he concentrated again on the block of fir.

"I wouldn't make a good patriarch after all," he said aloud. "Jacob worked seven years for his bride and I'm anxious about working for one more."

"What is it you're working for?" a familiar voice said as Caleb entered the shop behind Joseph.

"Oh, nothing, just mumbling to myself as I work. It passes the time away," Joseph explained, wondering how long Caleb had been behind him. "What brings you here, Caleb? I thought you were going to Tyre before coming home."

"I changed my plans," Caleb said as he turned a half-finished lamp stand over in his hands. "This is really quite good work, Joseph. I may yet convince you to supply me with some merchandise to take on my travels. Which is why I've come to talk to you."

Joseph eased his grip on his tools, standing as Caleb continued.

"You know I've been considering leaving Nazareth. Merchant

business passes through here well enough, but it's not the place to be, at least not for me."

"I know that, Caleb." Joseph reassured him. "I'm not even sure I want to stay here forever. But my options are limited."

"I don't know about that," Caleb said as he playfully swung the lamp stand at Joseph, just like they had teased each other as children. "You keep developing work like this and I'll be working for you!"

Caleb put down the lamp stand and steadied his voice. "When I leave Nazareth, I won't be taking Mary with me. She's a woman now and will have to pursue a life for herself."

"What's that got to do with me?" Joseph asked, trying not to show too much interest.

"Everything...if you want it to," volunteered Caleb. "I know I've been out of town a lot these past years, but I know you're interested in Mary. And if I read the signals from her, I think she's interested in you."

"All right," Joseph admitted. "We've talked. Quite a bit really. But I'm not ready...not yet. I need time to save money...and build a house...I couldn't bring her here."

Caleb glanced around the shop. "Well, I'm glad to hear that. But we do have a house. And when I'm gone it could be yours. We could make some sort of arrangement."

"We don't want to live in a house in town," Joseph countered, trying not to feel coerced by his friend into doing something he didn't want to. "Please don't misunderstand me, there's nothing wrong with the house. But it has a lot of painful memories that go with it. I think it would be better for Mary if we started out somewhere else."

"Fair enough," agreed Caleb. "I think my cousin Micah would

buy it from me. That way it would stay in the family; my father would want it that way. But that would leave Mary in an awkward position. She would end up a boarder in her cousin's house or have nowhere to go. However, if she were to be married soon..."

"How soon is soon?" Joseph interrupted.

Caleb pulled on his beard as he answered. "If Mary were to be betrothed, then I could sell the house to my cousin on the condition that Mary stay there until she is married. I get to relocate my business before the next busy season and in six months or so Mary moves to live with her husband and Micah gets his house. So the betrothal would have to be soon...and the marriage, well, soon enough."

Joseph laughed nervously. "Did you ever think when we were kids playing in the streets outside your house that we would one day be negotiating the sale of the house and the marriage of your sister?"

Caleb laughed without the slightest hesitation. "Actually," he said. "I think I did!"

The two friends grabbed each other by the shoulders and shared a laugh. Caleb picked up the lamp stand again and by reflex Joseph picked up the nearest stave of wood and the two men were back to being boys again, staging a mock sword fight that carried them out of the shop and into the street.

"So I guess I'll be paying your house a visit soon," Joseph suggested as Caleb surrendered.

"How soon is soon?" Caleb mocked Joseph's earlier question.

"I'll make sure Mary expects you for supper tonight. That's all the time I'm giving you to plan your next move."

"I wasn't planning on doing anything just an hour ago," Joseph responded with surprise in his voice. "Tell Mary I'm coming. I don't want to show up as a complete surprise."

"Good enough. I'll see if I can convince her to see you," Caleb joked. "See you later then, Joseph...I mean, brother!"

With a wave of his arm, Joseph bid farewell to Caleb and repositioned himself on his beam to resume his work. The mallet only struck the chisel three times before he was staring blankly down the street, lost in his thoughts. Excitement bubbled inside him at the idea of finally making his intentions for Mary public, but he was nervous. Was he really ready? Was she?

The sun was low enough to disappear behind the top of the shop door, signalling the end of the workday for Joseph. The time had come to wash up, change his clothes, and oil his beard. Tonight, he would betroth Mary and the life he dreamed of would finally begin.

Chapter Two
Betrothal

Mary made her way home from the market with her daily supplies, arms overloaded with a few cakes of flatbread, a clove of garlic, some onions, and a cruse of olive oil. Her face carried the freshness of youth though she had borne more pain than any sixteen year old woman should. A surprise gift from God four years after they had finally had a son, she was the child of her parent's old age and only twelve years old when they were both taken from her. A child no more, she had suddenly become a mother to her older brother Caleb and the mistress of their home.

None of these burdens had etched themselves onto her face. Her eyes still sparkled when she talked and her smooth cheeks hinted of dimples when she smiled. Dark hair cascaded over slender shoulders and tumbled down her back. She had cut her hair in mourning, but never since, vowing to let it grow until she was married. Her steps skipped with the spring of youth, yet she walked with an air of confidence and strength. Spending much of the time in Nazareth alone while her brother expanded his merchant business all the way to Jerusalem, she had to be strong.

Arriving at the house, she put her wares on the table beside the water jug and began to prepare the evening meal. Never knowing when to expect Caleb to be home, she always prepared enough for two. If Caleb didn't come home for supper, she would take the meal to one of the several widows who lived in town.

She would often deliver a meal to a widow who lived in the hills just outside Nazareth. Though it was an hour long journey there and back, she loved walking the paths through the hills. She learned this art of hospitality from her mother, who always set an extra place at the table. She would even invite the working men who had no wives to cook for them. More than once it was the father of her brother's friend, Joseph.

Joseph! How he had teased her as a small child, almost to the point of torment. But when her parents passed away, he had changed toward her. He was kind and thoughtful and even repaired items around the house that Caleb was neither willing nor able to do. Joseph was apprenticing as a carpenter; humble yet honest work. At least he had none of the wild aspirations of her brother. Caleb was far from settling down. His father had waited a long while before marrying and so would he. Perhaps Joseph was taking his cues from Caleb, for although they had talked about their future, he had never mentioned marriage.

They had talked about everything else, she mused as she prepared a sop with olive oil and wild herbs she had gathered on her last trek through the hills. They had talked of their mutual love of country life and living in the hills. He had told her of his desire to have a family. He had shown her some of his furniture designs and how he wished one day to craft items for use in the synagogue.

This was what she loved about Joseph more than anything else. He was a good man with ambitions to provide for his family. But his love for God and his longing to contribute to the spiritual life of the community drew her to him more than anything else. All of Mary's family on her mother's side were in the priesthood. She had visited them often as a child and was enthralled by their costumes and ceremony. From a little girl she had been taught how to sew the intricate garments that the Levites wore. She was now skilled in the arts of embroidery, tassels, and tunics.

There wasn't much opportunity for that kind of work in Nazareth and so she worked on mundane clothing and tablecloths. In her heart she longed for more opportunities to use her skill for the synagogue and temple. A man with the heart of Joseph would support her ambitions, and their mutual love for their religion would only enhance their life together.

"Mary!"

She almost spilled her bowl of olive oil as hands squeezed her shoulders from behind and turned her around.

"Caleb! You shouldn't sneak up on me like that. Just announce your arrival at the door like any decent person."

"But I'm not any decent person, you know," he teased, kissing her forehead. "I cut my trip short just to come home to have supper with you!"

"As you can see, it's all ready, at least what didn't spill on the table when you startled me. Come, let's sit down."

Caleb was only dipping his second piece of bread when he decided to inform Mary of his plans. "You know how I've been thinking of moving to Jerusalem," he began hesitantly. "I've decided that I'm going to move by the Feast of Tabernacles. I need time to get organized before the spring of next year."

"And you know I want you to take me with you," Mary countered.

"No, Mary. I'll be travelling as much as I do now, maybe more, and I won't be leaving you alone in a big city full of strangers."

"They are not all strangers. Jedidiah lives there, although I could not live with him. You know as well as I do that our cousins are priests and for weeks at a time they are in Jerusalem for temple duty."

"And for months at a time they are back at their homes in the hill country of Judea. I won't have it that way, Mary. I've seen too many single women in Jerusalem who are destitute, who shame themselves to survive. However," Caleb continued as she filled his cup with wine. "If you were married, then everything would change for you and you would be able to do as you wished. You could even stay here and raise your children in your father's house."

"This is hardly my father's house," Mary argued. "He only moved here when you were born. Besides, I would sooner live in the hill country." She cast a wistful gaze out the window to the hills beyond.

"That is entirely possible. I know Micah would buy the house from me. All you would have to do is find a husband who wants to live in the hills with you." He raised the cup of wine as he spoke, but set it back down without tasting it.

"I'm not looking for a husband, Caleb."

"You speak truly, for I think you have already found one!"

Mary stood up from the table and went to the window, gazing more intently at the hills while hiding her face from her brother. As she leaned on the window ledge she saw a figure approaching the house from the road. She gasped and clasped her cheeks as she turned quickly from the window and sprang to the back of the house, ducking behind the curtain that shielded her sleeping chamber.

"Mary, I'm sorry. I didn't mean to upset you so!" Caleb stood to follow after her.

"It's not you," she cried. "It's Joseph!"

Caleb turned as he heard the knock at the door. "So it is, Mary. I'm sorry. I forgot to tell you that he wanted to come over this evening. Forgive me, sister. I'll keep him company until you're ready to come out."

"Don't you answer the door until you answer me, Caleb!"

Caleb left the door untouched and moved closer to Mary's curtain as if to keep the conversation away from the man at the door. "What, Mary, what?"

"Have you talked to Joseph about marriage?"

"It is not just I who did the talking. Joseph has been talking as well. We're all old friends, Mary, and it was obvious that Joseph has feelings for you." He moved closer to the curtain as he whispered. "And I think you share the same feelings for him."

"Is that why he is here? Have you already made the arrangements Caleb? Answer me truthfully!"

"I have made no arrangements and discussed no price for your marriage, Mary. Honestly, I haven't. Even though as your older brother in the absence of our father, I could. In all my travels of late, believe me, I could have asked for and received a much higher price for you than a poor carpenter from Nazareth could ever afford."

"Caleb, how can you talk like that?"

"Because it's true! You've grown into a fine woman, my sister, and that is why I want you not to just go to the highest bidder, but spend your life with someone you also love. Someone who will treat you with dignity."

There was no reply from behind the curtain. Caleb thought he could hear a gentle sobbing and the occasional gasp of breath.

Caleb wished his parents were still alive; if only they had lived long enough to see Mary married and established on her own. It was the father's duty to negotiate the marriage of his daughter, entertain suitors, establish the bride price, and ensure a successful transition from his home to the groom's new home. Most fathers took it as a sacred responsibility while mothers spent their daughter's childhood schooling her in the arts of betrothal, marriage, and womanhood. Mary's time with her mother had been cut short, and Caleb had been a poor substitute as a father.

Now that Joseph was at the door, Mary probably felt like she had been set up, caught in a trap. The knocking echoed through the small house.

This should have been the happiest day of Mary's young life, when a husband-to-be came calling, standing at the door and knocking, waiting for the father to let him in. Upon entering, he would sip wine from the cup of betrothal offered by the father. Then the father would take it to the bride in private, and offer the cup to her. If she sipped from the cup, she was accepting the arrangements her father had made for her and was betrothed to her husband.

The whole family would then share a meal. The groom would return to his home and prepare the place where they would eventually live as husband and wife. The bride would continue to live with her parents, consecrating herself to the Lord and her new husband, and getting ready the clothing, bedding, and household goods she would need to begin her marriage. This preparation time could take months, even years. When the groom had everything ready at the new home, he would come to get her, almost by surprise. Only after the wedding feast would they begin to live together as husband and wife.

The knocking came at the door again.

"Answer the door, Caleb." Mary's voice was steady again.

"Are you sure, Mary?"

"You have the cup ready, don't you?" Mary challenged. "I've never known you to pour a cup of wine and not drink it."

"Honestly Mary, that wasn't why I asked you to pour a cup."

"You never asked me," Mary corrected him. "I poured it myself. And now I am ready to drink of that cup, if the Lord wills."

The knocking came at the door again. This time Caleb walked over to open the door. Joseph entered, looking older and more serious than he did hours before. He had changed into his best synagogue clothes. He even wore his prayer shawl. In his hand he cradled an object that he offered to Caleb.

Caleb unrolled the crude cloth in which it was folded. He almost dropped it as he held it up closer to his chest for a better look.

It was a small box, no bigger than a hand's length, four fingers in height and width. Constructed with strips of wood, it all fit together in the pattern of a star on each side. Intricate leather straps held the corners tight as the hinges and latch for the lid. In the centre of each star the wood had been hollowed out to hold a stone. None of the stones were precious, just the common colourful stones found throughout the Galilean hills, but each had been polished and oiled to bring out its beauty. Caleb recognized that the technique for inlaying the stones was the same Joseph used to weight the lamp stands he made. This signature trademark left no doubt who the artisan was.

"Joseph!" It was all Caleb could say as he opened the box to reveal seven compartments hollowed out of one block of wood, each rounded like a dish. Each one was a different size, and the smallest could hold a mite.

Caleb's gaze left the box to search Joseph's eyes which beamed pride and shame at the same time.

"It's a coin box," Joseph finally offered.

"It's a coin box worthy of a merchant, I trust."

Joseph was now looking past Caleb to the curtain which hid Mary. "No price would be high enough for Mary. Certainly nothing I could offer," Joseph admitted. "So I bring not a price, but a gift to an old friend."

Caleb searched for words to answer. "My father would have demanded a price for his daughter, I have no doubt. But I am under no such obligation. I am a merchant and trade with our people and foreigners for goods of every kind. I know the value of my sister and she is worth a price far above rubies. I suppose if someone were to suggest a price, I would chase him out of the house all the way to the Sea of Galilee."

While Caleb spoke he moved across the room and carefully placed the coin box on the table, covering it with the cloth. He grasped the cup of wine that had remained untouched, raising it with both hands as if to offer it to the heavens, then holding it out to Joseph as he stepped towards him.

Joseph took the cup with both hands, holding it gently as if he feared his rough hands would break it if he held it too tightly. He touched it to his lips and down again, his eyes never leaving the curtain, Raising the cup again to his mouth he took two drinks, enough to leave the cup half empty.

Caleb took the cup from Joseph and again, holding it high, walked over to the curtain, disappearing behind its folds. Joseph waited, barely inside the house yet, close enough to the door that he could feel it on his back, ready to make his exit if his proposal was refused. There was no sound from behind the curtain, only the rustle of the fabric as it moved in the breeze caused by the open door.

Finally the curtain parted and Caleb walked through with steady eyes.

Mary followed, eyes cast down to watch her own steps. Caleb motioned for Joseph to join them in the middle of the room, and as he moved towards them, Mary lifted her head. Her eyes held dark pools of moisture and her lips trembled.

As they neared each other, Caleb clasped each of their hands and held them together as he prayed. "Blessed art Thou, O Lord our God, King of the World, who has sanctified us by His Commandments, who sanctifies Israel by Chuppah and betrothal."

Caleb parted their hands and moved the benches around to offer Joseph the seat at the head of the table with Mary on his right. It was only as he sat down that Joseph noticed the cup of wine Caleb had placed in the centre of the table.

It was empty.

Chapter Three

The Visitor

The sun dipped below the highest hill as Mary started on her way down the hill. She would make it back to the town well before darkness set in over the neat white stone homes scattered in the valley encompassing the village of Nazareth.

She was returning from one of her self-imposed errands, bringing a meal to one of the widows who lived outside of town. She came here often, rarely staying as long as she had today, but her friend wanted to know about her betrothal and her new husband. Mary told her all she knew about his plans for their future, and she reassured her that as long as they were in Nazareth, she would be cared for.

To her right was the plot of land Joseph had talked about buying to build their home. She left the path and picked her way through the rocks to walk among its wildflowers and shrubs. The land tumbled down the hill towards town with numerous small ravines that trapped any rainwater. In these natural ditches Joseph planned to plant the trees he would harvest for his furniture building. Mary thought that these would be better put to use as a garden, but there was time for that discussion later.

She stopped on a rocky promontory and gazed at the town below.

This would be an excellent place to build a home; such a view it would have from every side. Large enough for Joseph to build a shop onto the house, like the one he worked in now, if that was what he wanted. Though not as dramatic as the hill country of Judea that she learned to love as a child, it was fertile and green, and she thought she could be quite content here.

Mary lingered too long on the hillside and darkness had fallen when she finally made it back inside the house. Caleb had left town again, this time to Caesarea Philippi to meet with some Greek traders in copper. He would be back tomorrow. She bolted the door, lit a lamp, and settled at the table to finish the embroidery on a priest's robe when a knock came at the door.

Mary set down her sewing and rose to answer the door, wondering who could be coming at this time of the evening. She intended to ask who it was before she unbolted the door, but the latch moved by itself. She reached to secure it but the door began to open. She jumped back, startled, thinking she would have to get Joseph to fix the latch.

A man stepped into the house and the door quietly closed behind him, though he made no gesture to shut it.

"Rejoice so highly favoured!" he greeted her. "The Lord is with you."

Mary was startled by these words and didn't understand what this greeting could mean. How is it this man entered her home without being invited? And what a thing to say! Rejoice? Rejoice that a stranger entered her home without an invitation? And then try to excuse impertinence by invoking the name of the Lord? *I surely hope the Lord is with me,* she thought, *for I do not know this man.*

But she could see this was no ordinary man. He was tall, probably a little taller than her brother. A robe just like the priest's garment she had just took to sewing covered him from shoulders to bare feet. Strange that he would wear such an intricate garment but have no sandals. His hair was not dark like the other men of Nazareth, but sandy like the Galilean seashore.

His face was finely featured, made more noticeable by the absence of a beard. The lamplight reflected in his eyes and she noticed that they were not dark but almost transparent. The colour of his eyes was whatever was reflected in them; dark in the shadows, fiery in the lamplight, and full of colour when he looked at her. The tone of his skin gave him a youthful appearance, and Mary could not tell whether he was older than Caleb or not. *Wearing a different garment and head scarf he could even be mistaken for a young woman,* she thought. But his voice betrayed him.

"Mary, do not be afraid; you have won God's favour," he said in a voice so convincing that she hesitated before objecting.

Surely the Lord is with me, she mused. *For though I am startled by his intrusion, I feel no fear of this man.*

"But I haven't been seeking God's favour, have I?" Mary dared to say out loud.

"Listen." He raised his hands to silence her.

She noticed that he wore no rings on his fingers and as he lowered his hands, she felt compelled to back up and sit on the bench.

The visitor moved closer to her, away from the door as if to guard their privacy.

His voice was tender yet serious. She had not heard such a tone since her father passed away. She listened as a good daughter would while the stranger continued.

"You are to conceive and bear a son, and you must name him Yeshua. He will be great and will be called Son of the Most High.

The Lord God will give him the throne of his ancestor David; he will rule over the House of Jacob forever and his reign will have no end."

Mary was dumbfounded. What was he saying? Was this what made her highly favoured? To have a Son of the Most High? Someone who will rule and reign forever? She had heard her father talk of the one who would one day rule over the House of David. All the Rabbis and priests expected the whole nation to be independent once again with its own leader, as they were in the glorious days of David and Solomon. Perhaps a king, or some thought a Messiah, to usher in the Day of the Lord. But what did that have to do with her?

She had to protest. She had never talked to anyone about her private life. Only mothers and daughters would ever discuss matters of sex and childbirth. Sometimes the talk at the village well and marketplace was peppered with talk of pregnancies and babies, but never in the company of the men, and certainly not with a man in private.

Only once had her father ever talked to her about childbirth. They were on the way home from one of their yearly Passover trips to Jerusalem. They had been joined there, as always, by her mother's relatives, most of whom were in the priesthood. That year, they stayed a few hour's walk west of Jerusalem in the hill country of Judea with Zechariah and Elisabeth. Zechariah was a priest in the division of Abijah and Elisabeth was her cousin, even though she was old enough to be her mother. It was there that Mary's love of the hill country was nourished. She and Caleb would play for hours among the rocks and trees, recreating whatever ancestral stories they could remember. Elisabeth fussed so much over them that they were reluctant to go back home to Nazareth.

"Elisabeth and Zechariah seem to like children, don't they,

Father?" Mary had asked on the way home.

"Yes, very much, I suppose," her father had answered.

"Why then don't they have children of their own?" Mary wondered. "Is it because Zechariah is a priest and is not allowed?"

"No, nothing like that," her father chose his words carefully. "Priests are allowed to take a wife and have children just like anyone else. If they didn't, then we would soon run out of priests. But Elisabeth has not been able to bear any children. Some think that it is a judgement from God." He tousled her hair with his rough hands as he teased. "I think having children may be more of a judgement from God than not having them."

"Maybe she's too old to have children anymore," Mary offered.

"What you say could be true," her father replied. "A woman only has so many years to bear children, and then she is barren. And Zechariah is not getting any younger either."

"It doesn't seem right that good people who want to have babies, and should have them, are not able," Mary protested.

"Now Mary," her father said. "I know how you get troubled about things and can't help thinking about them." He stopped walking and held her gently by the shoulders. "Whether we have children or not, we leave it to the wisdom of God. His ways are past finding out, and we must believe that whatever happens is the will of God for us." Her father's voice softened as he continued. "Someday, if God wills, you will get married and bear children of your own." He glanced away but quickly returned his eyes to her. "Or maybe not. You must learn to leave all of this to the will of God."

"I will, Father," Mary promised.

He nodded in approval and they continued their journey without speaking about it again.

Less than two years after that she lost him.

And now, the voice of the stranger, strangely mingled with the memory of her father, added to her bewilderment. Mustering the same courage to ask the tough questions she had as a child, Mary raised her objection. "But how can this come about, since I am a virgin?"

The stranger lifted his arms over his head and faced his palms towards her. The full sleeves of his robe created a canopy which trapped the light from the lamp, dancing on the inside folds of his now shimmering robe. The light reflected back to Mary with such intensity that she tried to look away, but could not.

"The Holy Spirit will come upon you," the stranger answered, "and the power of the Most High will cover you with its shadow. And so the child will be holy and will be called Son of God."

"But how can this come about?" Mary stammered her question again.

The visitor lowered his arms but kept his right palm near his face as he continued. "Know this too: your kinswoman Elisabeth has, in her old age, herself conceived a son, and she whom people called barren is now in her sixth month, for nothing is impossible to God."

Elisabeth? How does this stranger know Elisabeth? And how does he know she is with child? Impossible, Mary thought.

When Mary's mother passed away, it was Elisabeth who came to mourn with Mary, staying with her for weeks. Mary had taken the opportunity to continue the conversation she had with her father about Elisabeth being unable to bear children. Elisabeth had said that for years she was disappointed, but had finally resolved not to complain about it. She told Mary that even Zechariah had given up on having a child. Father had been right, after all. We must believe that whatever happens is the will of God for us.

"I am the handmaid of the Lord," said Mary, rising from the bench to look fully into the stranger's eyes. She wasn't convinced that what he said was true because she had no way of knowing. But at least she could find out if what he said about Elisabeth was true. If true for her cousin, then maybe it would be true for her.

She lowered her head in resignation. "Let what you have said be done to me."

Expecting a response, she looked up, but the room was empty. She checked the lamp and it was burning steady. Her embroidery still rested on the table. She went to check the door and found that it was latched. She opened it to see an empty street outside. Closing the door, she checked the latch, thinking that she would have to tell Joseph to come fix it.

"Joseph!" she gasped out loud. She would have to tell Joseph!

Chapter Four
Ponderings

Mary didn't know what to do. The stranger had disappeared and she was alone again. She returned to her embroidery but could not bear to work on a robe that looked exactly like the one the visitor wore. After dropping several stitches, she trimmed the lamp and went to her mat.

She drifted in and out of slumber. The memory of her father's voice somehow made the visit of the stranger even more confusing. She wondered what it all could mean, and as the night dragged on, she wondered if it really happened at all. It didn't help that Caleb was out of town. If he had been home, then maybe the whole encounter wouldn't have happened.

Mary had always been introspective, preferring to quietly reflect on the events of her life rather than discussing them with others. When her parents died she found it hard to talk to anyone about it. It took her a long time to process what had happened, and it was months before she could talk even openly about it with Caleb.

Now she had another incredible situation to mull over. She was going to be with child. But how? And when? How would she know it was really happening? She would have to tell Joseph, but there was no way she could! How could she tell him that she was going to have a child that wasn't his? And what about Caleb? What would he think of his yet unwed sister having a child? It would bring a horrible shame to them all.

Morning came after little sleep and Mary attempted to quiet her racing mind and spirit by keeping her hands busy. After finishing her morning chores, she walked to the market but went through her routine in a daze. The only thing she could concentrate on was avoiding any place where she might run into Joseph.

Thankfully, Caleb was expected home that day so she spent the afternoon giving the house a thorough cleaning and baking fresh cakes for their evening meal. Several times she tried the latch on the door, half expecting it to be faulty, but each time finding there was nothing wrong with it. She was still preparing the meal when her thoughts turned from her own predicament to Elisabeth.

Imagine! Elisabeth at her age, now six months pregnant! She and Zechariah would be old enough to be the child's grandparents.

They had always found time to spend with her and Caleb. Zechariah was fond of not just telling, but acting out all the great stories of the prophets of old.

One day they would find large flat stones and be Moses with the Ten Commandments. They next day they would be David taking aim with their slings. Whenever there were rocks to move about, they were Nehemiah building up the walls of Jerusalem. Elisabeth's favourite was to dress Mary up in her finest linens and whatever jewelry she could find and parade her about as Queen Esther. Mary hoped Elisabeth carried a boy, for she would certainly spoil a girl.

Mary paused as she realized her daydreaming gave her the answer to her problem. If Elisabeth expected a child as the stranger said, then she must find out at once if it was true. Surely, in her sixth month, everyone would know about it. Sooner or later, news would reach her and Caleb, but they had heard nothing about this. Maybe the stranger visited Elisabeth and that is how he knew she was expecting. There were just so many questions and Elisabeth was the only one who could give her the answers.

The sky darkened and Mary wondered what was keeping Caleb so long, but felt glad for the chance to formulate her plan. She would have to journey to Elisabeth's home in the hill country of Judea. Even though she was capable, making the journey alone was out of the question. Solo travelling over several nights was not something a respectable young woman would do. And now that she was betrothed to Joseph, he would never allow it. She wished for a moment that was the only thing she would ever have to explain to Joseph, but pushed those thoughts to the back of her mind as she continued to plan.

Maybe she could convince Caleb to take her with him on one of his trading expeditions. Often Caleb would take trips to Jerusalem, about three days journey. Once there, she could make it herself the few hours more to Elisabeth's home. She had been there often enough, and would easily make it to their village before dark. Since she was betrothed to Joseph and had no mother to help her sew her wedding garments and other things brides were expected to have ready, she could legitimately use Elisabeth's advice and help. Joseph was busy getting his affairs in order and would not miss her too much. Besides, it was not unusual for the groom to spend very little time with his betrothed until the wedding day. If Elisabeth was indeed expecting, then a visit to help her would be all the more appropriate.

She would just have to be careful not to mention that she thought Elisabeth was expecting. Caleb would want to know why she would think such a ridiculous thought. She couldn't tell him, or Joseph, at least not yet. Mary needed to keep the visit of the stranger to herself until she could confirm what he had told her about Elisabeth. If what he said turned out not to be true and Elisabeth was still barren, then she would not believe anything else he said. She could even assume it had only happened in her own imagination. And if it turned out that Elisabeth was already six months pregnant, then at least Mary would have a sympathetic ear to hear her story and sort out what it all meant.

A knock came at the door.

"Mary!"

Caleb was home! She hurried to answer it but hesitated when she went to undo the latch. All the events of yesterday evening, her restless sleep and her pondering all day long raced through her mind. Her hands were on the latch, but couldn't move.

"Mary? Open the door!" Caleb's voice sounded worried.

Mary fumbled with the latch and Caleb pushed the door inward, his arms full of blankets, jars, and purses of every kind. He unloaded his goods on the table as Mary closed the door.

"I'm sorry, Caleb. You always told me to keep it latched when I'm at home alone at night, and so I did."

And with that explanation, she fell into his arms, sobbing.

Chapter Five
The Plan

Despite her turmoil, Mary slept soundly that night. Having Caleb at home on his mat made her feel secure. She wondered how much better it would be to have Joseph at her side every night. But just the idea of Joseph filled her with such uncertainty that she had to push those thoughts to the back of her mind.

Caleb hadn't asked much about her tearful outburst the night before and she was relieved he was home. He claimed he never really understood women, and most of the time she agreed.

They had eaten their late meal quietly while Caleb talked of his trip to Caesarea Philippi and all the new merchants he had traded with. Mary had made no mention of her plans to visit Elisabeth, choosing to wait until Caleb told her where he was off to next. She didn't have to wait long.

She had just put the morning meal on the table when Caleb started to talk of his next journey. He had done well with the copper traders and brought back several items of interest: small bowls, cups, even jewelry, but nothing that would sell very well in a small town like Nazareth. He wanted to try to market them in a larger city where people with more wealth and leisure could appreciate them.

When Caleb suggested Jerusalem, Mary tried to conceal her eagerness. "I would like to go with you, Caleb."

"Now why would you want to do that? What would you do there?"

"I was thinking, while you were gone, that I would like to visit our cousin Elisabeth."

"We just saw them last Passover," Caleb objected.

"I know. But since then, I have become betrothed. Or have you forgotten, my dear brother?" Mary teased as she slid the coin box that Joseph had made across the table towards him.

"I have not forgotten. You wouldn't let me. Nor would Joseph, I am sure. If you are so hopelessly betrothed," Caleb teased her in return as he opened the coin box, "why are you so anxious to get away from him?"

"I'm not!" she exclaimed, surprising herself with the emotion she felt. "I don't expect you to understand the ways of women, Caleb," Mary said. "But there are many things a bride must prepare for her wedding, and I have no kinswoman here in Nazareth to help me."

"No kinswoman, perhaps, but several women you have been kind to over the years that would be only too glad to help you," Caleb countered.

"I suppose that is true," Mary tried to agree and not seem too anxious to pursue her objective. "But none know me as Elisabeth does. No one else can give me the kind of advice and help my own mother would have."

The mention of their mother made Caleb look admiringly at the wares spread over the table. He picked up each one and turned it over in his hands: a silk head piece with an embroidery of golden thread, a copper plate that was shiny enough to reflect an image, a ring so delicate that it would be fit for a queen.

"Our parents would have appreciated goods of this quality, Mary." Caleb sighed at their memory.

"I'm sure they would have been proud to have had any one of them," Mary said approvingly. "But not as proud as they would be of the fine merchant their son has become." She reached across the table to hold the plate so that it reflected his face.

"Well," Caleb said. "If I am such a good merchant then I should at least be as good a brother and honour my sister's requests. How many days do you need to get ready?"

His quick response surprised Mary. She rose from her place at the table and wrapped her arms around his neck.

"Now don't start crying again," Caleb cautioned.

"I'll try not to." Mary's voice cracked with emotion.

"Women!" Caleb said. "They're always crying!"

"Only for joy, my dear brother. Only for joy that you've taken such good care of me." Mary kissed his hair and went back to the table to finish cleaning up as Caleb finished his meal.

The next morning, Mary was ready to answer him. "I would like to finish the embroidery on the priest's robe that I was working on yesterday," she said as she cleared the table of the growing pile of goods Caleb was bringing out of his storage chest. "If you manage to stay out of my way today I could have it ready before the Sabbath. Then we could leave early the first day of the week."

"That would work for me. A couple days at home should be long enough to gather up a few more samples of goods to take with me. I would almost have enough to justify arranging for a donkey for us. What would you think of that?"

"Well, don't do it on my account. I don't mind the walking, as long as you don't make me carry your burdens for you," Mary cautioned him. "I'll have enough of my own belongings to look after."

"Don't you worry about that. I've taken this journey more times than I care to remember by myself. And don't forget, you're the one who asked to go," he reminded her as he headed to the door. Caleb's hand moved to the latch, pausing as he fumbled with it. "You will have to tell Joseph," Caleb instructed.

"Joseph?" Mary tried to hide the emotion in her voice as she stared at the door. The events of the last two days flooded her mind. The visit of the stranger, his spectacular visage and message, the memories of her father, and her questions about Elisabeth.

"Yes, Joseph. You had a hard time working this latch last night, and it doesn't seem much better today."

"Oh, the latch!" Mary was thankful he didn't notice the relief in her voice.

"By the way, Mary, you should let him know what your plans are." Caleb paused in the doorway. "He'll worry about you all the while you're gone, I'm sure."

"I will" Mary confirmed. "I'll stop by to see him after I go to the market. I will expect you home for the evening meal, and not as late as last night, Caleb," she warned as he started down the street, waving her last words off with both hands.

Mary closed the door and leaned against it for a minute to collect her thoughts. *Surely the Lord is with me,* she thought as she gathered her baskets and left for the market. *Caleb has agreed so readily to take me to Jerusalem. I pray Joseph is as understanding.*

Chapter Six
Joseph Agrees

Joseph picked his way down the hill, imagining the path he would soon have to choose to lead to his new home. The meeting with the landowner went as well as could be expected. He had explained his betrothal and marriage plans but was not able to negotiate a lower price. The owner however, intrigued by his plans to grow trees on the land, offered to let Joseph gather the rocks he would need to build his house off his land in exchange for planting trees on his new plot. This would save Joseph some time and money in getting his building project off the ground, and go a long way towards building a good relationship with his new neighbour.

He was still concerned about the total cost of building the home. It would be small at first, just one room. Later, he could build a shop on the back. He had made the plans and built the one he worked at now and thought it a very functional space.

Of course, he would have to plan for the arrival of children. While they were young, they would just fit into whatever space was available. As they grew, he would have time to add on to the house again, if needed. And since they would be living in the country, there would lots of room for them to run around. Besides, he thought, both he and Mary were from small families so having a large family was not expected.

In fact, Joseph realized as he arrived back into town and dodged around some boys playing in the street, he had never thought too much about children. He had a happy childhood but was thrust into manhood when his father passed away. He occasionally helped out at the synagogue with the young boys but hadn't spent a lot of time with children. He assumed Mary was more experienced than he. They hadn't talked a lot about children except that the Lord would send some along eventually and they would deal with it when the time came.

Walking up the street to the shop, Joseph noticed how plain the homes were in Nazareth. Tidy enough and functional, but lacking in colour and variety. The home he would build would be unique. He would lengthen the roof beams so they overhung the wall to create some shade and a place to hang tools, utensils, and plants. His windows would be lower to let in more light and allow one to see outside while at the table.

He would extend the stone wall past the outside corner of the house with steps of stone to create a courtyard for privacy and a garden. On the inside he would wedge wooden planks to protrude from the stone wall to hold candles and lamps. He would make a home like no other for Mary and she would be the talk of the town.

Just as he turned the final corner, he saw Mary coming towards him. She carried two baskets laden with bread and fruit from the market. Though she was dressed the same as the other women in town, there was something about the way she carried herself and the glow from her youthful face that always made him conscious of his own appearance. Joseph glanced at his own clothing and quickly dusted himself off, hoping that his hair was not too windblown from his walk.

He hid his pleasure at this impromptu visit. "Mary, what are you doing up here at this time of day?"

"I delivered five loaves and two fish to a widow, and we were just talking," Mary said. "You know, all the kinds of things that men are not interested in." She smiled, knowing he wouldn't challenge her on that.

"Sorry I asked," Joseph pretended to apologize.

"Actually, I came to talk to you. Do you have to go back to the shop or can you walk me home?"

"I do have to go back to the shop, and I believe the way goes right past the house of one Caleb and his beloved sister Mary." Joseph laughed as he took one of the baskets from her and turned to head back down the street the way he came.

That is what Mary loved so much about Joseph. Hardly a man in Nazareth would be caught carrying a woman's market basket. But Joseph would. This man whose hands shaped, and were shaped, by wood and stone was not too proud to help a woman carry her baskets.

"Caleb is back from Caesarea Philippi and is going to Jerusalem next," Mary began.

"I'm not surprised," Joseph said. "I know he eventually wants to set up his merchant business there."

"Yes, he does," Mary agreed. "And I would like to go with him."

"Really? Why?" Joseph asked. "What would you do there? Is it even safe there in the big city?"

"You men are all alike," Mary lectured. "Caleb said the same thing. I am not staying in Jerusalem. I would be going to visit my cousin Elisabeth who lives in the hill country just a few hours to the west."

"Elisabeth? The relatives Caleb always talks about when in Jerusalem for the Passover?" Joseph questioned.

"That's right. She was the one who came to stay with us after our mother died," Mary explained. "She could help me with many of the things I must prepare for as a bride. You know, all the things you men are not supposed to know about."

"Believe me, Mary," Joseph said. "I do not know, nor do I want to. But how long will you be gone?"

"I don't really know. A lot depends on Elisabeth. Her husband Zechariah is a priest and I don't really remember whether he is on duty this time of year," Mary explained. "I think I would be gone three or four Sabbaths."

"What does Caleb think of all this?" Joseph asked.

"He's happy to have me come along. I think he'll be treating me as one of his beasts of burden." Mary laughed at the thought.

"I'll be a beast of a burden to him if I find out he has," Joseph warned with a smile in his voice. "Of course, I'll miss you, Mary. But I suppose I shouldn't be seeing you too often in any case. Maybe it's better you are far away so you don't distract me from my work."

"Like I am today?" Mary smiled at him.

"Like today, yes." Joseph laughed. "And from my real work of getting a home ready for us to live in. I don't even know if it's proper for me to tell you, but just today I've arranged to purchase a plot of land in the north hill, the one I was telling you about." Joseph searched her face for a reaction, but couldn't tell if she was surprised or not. "I could use the time you're away to start clearing the land and piling the rocks for the house," Joseph said. "By the time you get back, I might even have a clearing levelled."

"That would be wonderful, Joseph," Mary said as they approached her house. "Maybe I can convince Caleb to trade for some cloth in Jerusalem and I can start sewing." Mary's voice faltered as the sight of her door flooded her mind with the visit of the stranger and the items she would have to sew if the stranger's words came true.

"Sewing what?" Joseph asked as he put the basket down outside the door. "Oh, I get it. Sewing things that I'm not supposed to know about," Joseph teased. "Let me tell you, Mary—we grooms have a few secrets of our own, you know."

"I'm sure you do," Mary agreed quickly, hoping to end the conversation on a different subject. "Thanks for walking me home. I'll ask Caleb to be sure to see you before we leave. We'll all have supper together on the Sabbath before we leave, if you'd like," Mary offered.

"I'd like that very much. Suppers at the house of Caleb and Mary have been very kind to me lately," Joseph said, and before she could stop him he reached to unlatch the door. Mary quickly stooped to pick up the basket Joseph had put down, forcing herself not to watch as he unlatched the door.

"There's something wrong with this latch, Mary," Joseph said as he twisted it in his hand. "You should have told me and I would have fixed it for you."

"I know," Mary offered weakly as she stood up to enter the doorway. "I should have told you, Joseph. Goodbye." It was all she was able to say as she walked through the doorway.

"I'll see you soon, Mary," Joseph called out as he headed down the street the way they had come.

Mary put her baskets on the table and went back to the doorway to watch him walk away. *What a kind and generous man,* she thought. *Willing to let me go away to spend time with relatives.* Rather than complain about her leaving, he was happy to have more time to spend preparing a home for her. What if she finds out Elisabeth is pregnant and that means she will be too? How could she bring any shame on this man? How could she burden him with a child that was not his own? Suddenly feeling weak, she leaned against the door and her hand settled upon the latch.

"I should have told you," she said aloud, knowing that Joseph was too far away to catch her voice, at the same time wondering if the strange visitor was close enough to hear.

"I should have told you, Joseph," she again, tears tracing a path down her cheek.

Chapter Seven
Sabbath Day

The next few days passed quickly. Mary kept busy finishing the embroidery on the priest's garment, doing it as fast as possible. Everything about it reminded her of her visitor and the robe he wore which was so similar to the one she was working on. She was never so happy to have something finished and out of her sight.

Caleb was busy as well getting ready for the trip to Jerusalem. He had arranged for a donkey to carry his goods, so Mary was able to pack a few supplies so she could do some sewing with Elisabeth. She hoped Caleb would let her go to the market in Jerusalem and find some material for her wedding. Elisabeth could help her with that, she was sure.

Finally, the Sabbath came. Early that morning, she and Caleb went to the Synagogue as had been their custom since they were children. Their father had always sat in the seats reserved for the leaders of the synagogue. Because he had married into a family of priests, he had been held in high esteem among the synagogue community.

Readings from the Scriptures were assigned to the eldest representative from each family for the year. Today was Caleb's turn, and Mary hoped he would do at least an adequate job. Many hoped that Caleb would follow in his father's footsteps, but Caleb was more interested in complexities of trade than the interpretation of the Torah.

At the synagogue, Mary sat with the other women in their designated section. Taking no part in the service, they were passive listeners as the men read selections from the Law, Psalms, and the Prophets. Occasionally, a visiting rabbi would be invited to expound on the reading of the day, engaging a local man to comment on the application of his interpretation.

To many women, synagogue attendance was a tedious ritual. The talk at the village market the next day would be spiced with their complaints of the way the men would manipulate the reading to their advantage. That is why the men do not allow the girls to go to school, they would reason. Then they would be able to read for themselves and challenge the men and their ways. Even without schooling, many of the women had remarkable memories and could tell the stories of their ancestors and their writings with stunning clarity.

Mary was among them. Not only had she listened with strict attention at the synagogue, but she enjoyed engaging her father with discussions at home. Early on, her father would chide her for thinking about things too much, but he secretly delighted in her curiosity. So much so, that he taught Mary to read, much to her mother's displeasure. Mary read everything her father could get his hands on, and after his death, it was she, not Caleb, who treasured his few parchments of the Torah and Psalms.

The morning at the synagogue passed without incident, until it came time for Caleb to stand and go to the reading table. Mary was thrilled for him. It was an honour to be called upon, and it signalled the growing respect that Caleb was getting from the townspeople.

Caleb rose from his seat beside Joseph and walked to the table. Mary could only see the back of Joseph, but he seemed to straighten up on his bench as if he too was proud of his best friend. Glancing first in her direction, Caleb took the parchment and began to read.

"From the book of the prophet Isaiah." Caleb's voice was confident, and Mary smiled at how he read with a rabbinical flair just as their father had.

"Again the Lord spoke to Ahaz. Ask a sign of the Lord your God; Let it be deep as Sheol or high as heaven. But Ahaz said, I will not ask and I will not put the Lord to the test. And he said, Hear then, O house of David! Is it too little for you to weary men, that you weary my God also? Therefore the Lord himself will give you a sign. Behold, the virgin will conceive and bear a son, and will call his name Immanuel."

Caleb continued to read, but the rest of the words were unintelligible to Mary's racing mind. Whether she had ever heard or read this passage before, she couldn't remember. But she was quite certain that she would never forget what she was hearing. *"A virgin will conceive."* Why this passage, and why now, and being read by her own brother? She could almost hear her father cautioning her, *"Mary, you think too much."* But how could she not?

The strange visitor to her home just days ago gave her the same message as this prophecy written hundreds of years before. She would be with child even though she had never been with a man. Her hands began to shake and she clasped them together, hoping the other women would not notice as her whole body began to tremble.

Caleb finished the reading and handed the parchment back. Taking his seat, he searched Mary's eyes for approval. But Mary's head was down as her clasped hands cupped to catch tears she could not stop. The remainder of the service with its commentary and readings were inaudible to her. All she heard were the voices of her brother, the stranger, and her father.

"A virgin will conceive."
"You will be with child."
"Mary, you think too much."
"A virgin will conceive."
"You will be with child."
"Mary, you think too much."

Why did this have to happen to her? Just when her brother was gaining the respect he deserved in the community, would she shame him and the memory of her father by having a child without a husband? And what of Joseph? What would happen to his reputation? And how could their betrothal possibly continue?

The voices in her head were so overwhelming, she wondered if the women around her could hear them as well. Breaking all protocol, she left the synagogue before the men were even finished speaking. She had to escape before Caleb and Joseph left so she could go home to wash her face and appear as fresh and composed as possible. She couldn't bear them questioning her about anything right now.

As she arrived home, she paused as she reached for the door latch. *Will I ever be able to open this door without reliving that night?* her heart cried out.

Suddenly she was overcome with the desire to escape, to never have to use this door latch, to never enter the house, to never face the people of this town again. Her parents were gone. Caleb would soon be leaving for the city, and her future with Joseph was in jeopardy.

What she wouldn't give right then for a fresh start. To put it all behind her and start again, somewhere else, even as someone else. She released the latch and entered the house. Tomorrow could not come soon enough.

She washed her faced repeatedly, wishing the water was colder so her eyes would not be puffy. Just as she finished putting the meal on the table, Caleb and Joseph burst through the door, joking with each other.

"Mary, I don't know if I can continue with our betrothal," Joseph said.

Mary's heart jumped. "Why not?"

"Because," Joseph explained, "I don't know if I can be a brother to the learned rabbi Caleb of Nazareth."

"Don't you fear," countered Caleb. "Even esteemed rabbis can count illiterate carpenters among their family relations."

"Oh, stop it you two," Mary pretended to scold them, secretly thankful they hadn't noticed her early exit from the synagogue.

"If I was illiterate, I wouldn't have noticed how poorly you read," Joseph countered.

"Sit down and put some food in your mouths," Mary ordered them. "Maybe that will stop your childish jabbering,"

"So, you're not happy with your brother's reading today, dear sister?" Caleb continued the joking as they sat down.

"Of course I am, Caleb," Mary tried to be serious. "While you were reading, I was thinking of Father and how proud he would be of you."

"Oh yes." Caleb's voice lost some of its frivolity. "I will never be able to replace Father. I'm afraid I will never do much more at the synagogue than I did today."

"I would be afraid for our synagogue if you did," Joseph teased.

"I would be afraid if we spent our last day together talking nonsense," Mary scolded them again.

"Mary's right," Caleb agreed. "You two should be talking about what will be happening when Mary gets back. I expect my cousin Micah will be wanting the house once spring comes, so I wouldn't want to see any delays in your wedding plans."

With that, the conversation turned to their journey to Jerusalem, the plans to get Mary safely to Elisabeth's, how soon she would return, and all the assorted details that Joseph, always the long term planner, wanted to know. Caleb busied himself with some notes at the table, kindly giving Mary and Joseph some time alone.

Darkness had fallen by the time Joseph said his final farewell to Mary. He promised again to start preparing the land for their home, and even started to describe some of the furniture he would work on in the evenings, when Mary stopped him.

"Joseph, you shouldn't do too much. You have your jobs for Obadiah to finish and everything else. We'll not have a good start if you spend all your time preparing for us and find out you've lost your job."

"Don't worry, Mary," Joseph reassured her. "That's why it will be good for you to go away for a few weeks. The time I would spend with you I can spend doing things for you."

"That's good of you, Joseph, but there's still so much we don't know, so much that could happen," she pleaded with him, testing his resolve.

"Nothing could happen that could change things for us, Mary."

"Are you so sure?"

"Your father was right. You think too much." Joseph stroked her face with his rough hands and let himself out the door.

"Mary?"

She turned to see Caleb gazing at her intently.

"I see you've been far too busy getting ready for this trip. You're going to drive poor Joseph mad with your questions."

"But Caleb, you don't understand," Mary started to defend herself.

"Yes, I do," Caleb cut her off. "Joseph is mad enough about you already. Nothing you could say or do could change that. Now you better get some sleep, we will be starting out at first light."

"Caleb," Mary started again, but her voice cracked and faltered.

"Now don't start crying, Mary," Caleb held her by the shoulders. "You'll be back home before you know it and everything is going to work out just fine."

Too tired to resist, Mary nodded her head and held back her tears. She retired to her mat, wondering if the journey she began the next day would be one that would ever her lead her back to Nazareth and her life with Joseph.

Chapter Eight
The Journey

The road leading east from Nazareth towards the Sea of Galilee was a popular route used by the caravans of traders travelling towards Damascus and returning from the ports of the Mediterranean. Often narrow and rocky, it descended through the hills until it merged with the north-south route from Damascus to Jerusalem.

Caleb had arranged for a donkey to travel with them and on this beast were his sacks of goods for trading in Jerusalem, the baskets of food Mary had prepared, a few cooking utensils, and a small makeshift tent for the three nights they would spend on the road. Caleb carried his own personal belongings, including the coin box that Joseph had made him, as he led the donkey. Mary walked dutifully behind, carrying her own clothing and a jug they would use for fresh water along the way.

It was along this route that Mary and Caleb travelled at least once a year with their parents to the feasts in Jerusalem. These frequent trips established a predictable routine for the journey. They started out as soon as dawn broke, with only some bread from the day before to calm their appetite. As they met other travellers along the way, they would walk with them for a while to determine if the pace was suitable. If it was, they would journey together, knowing it was safer to travel together than by themselves, especially as evening approached.

Once part of a group, they would generally stay together until their various destinations were reached. They would water their animals at the same time, stopping to eat and refresh themselves as a group. They would often share each other's burdens and the evening meal would be a communal affair. Mary was sure that Caleb's sense of adventure and skill at trading was developed on these journeys. Once, as a boy, he went missing for a whole day, finally showing up at the evening meal just as their parents were about to go back down the road looking for him. He had spent the day with a large family from Egypt, somehow communicating as children do through play rather than language.

It was not yet the sixth hour of the day when they attached themselves to such a caravan of travellers on their way to Jericho, Jerusalem, and beyond. The group already included textile merchants who had landed at Caesarea Philippi, families from Capernaum and Beersheba. They were a diverse group and she was glad none of the families were from Nazareth. Caleb spent his day bartering with the merchants, occasionally checking with Mary who walked with the smaller group of women and children.

Their first night's stop was at the Sea of Galilee. There the east-west road they travelled intersected a road that followed the Jordan River valley to Jericho. There was no village khan to stay at, so they pitched their tent to secure their belongings and they made a simple meal on an open fire. Mary retired before nightfall while Caleb walked to the seashore to watch the fishermen prepare their boats and nets for a night of fishing.

As the caravan broke camp in the morning and prepared to leave, they were joined by some of the Galileans who were journeying to Jerusalem. These fishermen were not travelling with their families, and their rough demeanour made Mary uneasy. Joseph was a rough and tumble carpenter, but not crude as these men seemed to be. She was glad that Caleb was accompanying her.

They stopped at midday to rest and refresh themselves. As the afternoon waned, the men decided to rest for the evening at the village of Aenon. Khans were of various types, depending on the size of village that provided them. Larger towns would select a site on the edge of town and build a stone wall in a square outline for protection from the roadway. Within the wall stone stalls would be built high enough to shelter a donkey or camel. Above these animal enclosures would be a wooden floor for the travellers to put their burdens and roll out their sleeping mats. In the open courtyard between the stalls there would be a well or cistern and a stone pit where fires for cooking could be kindled.

Khans such as this offered protection and relief for travellers and their animals. Communities provided these khans to promote trade at their local markets and to keep travellers from otherwise inconveniencing the townspeople as they sought places to camp and house their animals. Robbery and other crimes were also less likely to happen when travellers were grouped together. Enterprising individuals in the larger towns and cities would build an inn attached to the khan where the wealthy could hire servants to attend to their animals while they enjoyed private lodging.

Theirs was the only caravan at the khan that night and Caleb and Mary were able to secure their own private stall for their donkey and themselves. They had eaten the bread Mary brought along during the day and so Mary set about to prepare an evening meal of vegetables. She had barely started when Caleb appeared with two fish he had bartered for with the fishermen.

By the time they finished their meal, darkness had fallen, so Mary retired to her sleeping mat in the stall. Tired yet excited that she was now only a couple days away from Elisabeth and the answers she hoped to find there, she fell asleep to the sound of Caleb bickering with the other men around the fire late into the night.

The next day's journey began without incident. The terrain was dry and Mary grew weary of the dust that she shuffled through as they followed the men. Towards midday, one of the children of the family from Capernaum began to complain of sore feet. He was only about five years old and had no sandals to protect him from the stony road. His parents were already burdened with their loads and a smaller girl whom they half carried, half dragged along with them. Mary convinced Caleb to let her put her water jug and sewing material on the donkey and offered to carry the boy as far as she was able.

On many of their trips to Jerusalem, Mary had begged her father to carry her at least one mile. Her father rarely refused and Mary remembered how he would boost her onto his shoulders and she would bounce along the road, oblivious to the strain she was adding to her father's stride. After a mile, her mother would try to convince her to walk on her own again, but her father would protest.

"She asked for one mile, but I'm sure I can carry her two," her father would say. "Someday she will be too big to ask, and I will be too old to oblige."

With that, her father would take her off his shoulders and make a sort of sling with his cloak that hung around his shoulders creating a pocket around his back. He would position Mary in the pocket so her legs could squeeze his waist and her arms could hang loosely around his neck and shoulders. With the change of her weight on his body, he could easily carry her another mile, tickling her toes to tease or torment her.

With these memories flooding her mind, Mary boosted the lad onto her shoulders and continued their journey. Although it wasn't too long before Mary started to feel the discomfort of her extra burden, she was glad for the distraction. Keeping the child amused by commenting on all the birds, flowers, and landscapes they passed kept Mary's mind off the questions that had prompted this journey in the first place. Besides, if any of the things she was told were to come true, she might as well get used to having to deal with a child.

After a brief stop for water, the men decided to travel another hour or so. Mary grabbed some of her sewing material and quickly tied a sling much like the one her father had fashioned out of his cloak. This time she offered to carry the younger girl, much to the relief of the parents. As they walked the last couple hours to their next stop, Mary was glad she had a much lighter, quieter child. She wondered if that was what it would be like to carry her own child in her body.

At last, they reached the khan outside Jericho. In gratitude for her help, the family from Capernaum offered to make supper for her and Caleb, which they gladly accepted. Retiring immediately after the meal, Mary fell asleep without even hearing Caleb bartering by the fire.

After an early start, they made the final climb into the holy city of Jerusalem. This climb had always made her nervous. The city was so much larger than Nazareth, and people bustled and jostled in every direction. The smells of the city were overwhelming; the smoke of a thousand cooking fires, the fragrance of the markets, the stench of cattle and camels and sheep.

Her pre-occupation with her mission made her unaware of these distractions this time. Their party broke up as they walked the crowded streets until she and Caleb were alone. It was well into the afternoon before they came to their uncle's home where they would spend the night before she left on her own for Elisabeth's. They had stayed there often, as had Elisabeth and Zechariah when Zechariah was on temple duty. Once they had all stayed there together in a riot of kids and animals and adults. *When had Elisabeth been here last?* Mary wondered. *Does anyone know she is expecting, and should I say anything?* Mary prayed they would all be so distracted by their visit that she could avoid the whole matter for this one evening.

Uncle Jedadiah's home was a big stone house on a rise of land that provided a good view of the temple courtyard from the upper room where Mary retired to immediately after the evening meal. Her obvious tiredness allowed her to escape the others with only a few questions about her betrothal to Joseph and subsequent trip to visit Elisabeth. None of the conversation required her to comment on her knowledge of Elisabeth's condition, and certainly not her own. She was staring out the window of her room as the evening light changed the colour of the temple walls from a greyish-white to a simmering salmon when Caleb interrupted her thoughts.

"Not sleeping yet?" he pretended to scold her.

"No," she sighed. "I was just remembering all the times we have come to Jerusalem and how this time it feels so different."

"Different?" Caleb questioned her mood.

"Yes. You're thinking of moving here permanently now." Her gaze never left the temple. "Perhaps never returning to Nazareth.

And my life, it's..." She couldn't finish

"It's going to be fine," he reassured her, hugging her from behind. "Joseph is a good man and you will have a wonderful life together. He'll build you a home and you will have children who will rise up to call you blessed." He felt her trembling, and dampness on his arm. "Mary? What's wrong? Are you crying again?" He turned her around to wipe the tears from her face.

"It's about children, and being with child," Mary was sobbing now.

"Are you afraid you won't be able to have children?" Caleb asked with a growing concern in his voice. "What do you know that you haven't told me?"

"Plenty," Mary sobbed. She could not hold her secret in any longer, and realized now that they were in Jerusalem, Caleb would not be able to talk to Joseph for some time, and by the time he did, it wouldn't matter.

Caleb held her face in his hands and searched her eyes. "What great secrets do you ponder in that heart of yours, Mary?" Caleb mimicked his father's tone.

"Did I tell you, Caleb, why I had to go see Elisabeth?" Caleb's technique had worked its magic on her as her voice steadied.

"You said she would help you prepare for your wedding. She will be a big help, I'm sure," Caleb reassured her.

"She will," Mary agreed. "But there's something else." Maybe if she told him about Elisabeth first, it would ease the conversation into her own condition. "Elisabeth is expecting a child."

"Elisabeth?" Caleb laughed. "Zechariah is old enough to be a grandfather!"

"I know," Mary agreed, allowing Caleb's laughter to relax her.

"But she is expecting, at least I think she is."

"You think?" Caleb was still laughing. "Who told you? Uncle Zedadiah? Or did you hear gossip around the village well all the way back in Nazareth?"

"No, nothing like that. You know I don't listen to idle chatter, Caleb," Mary defended herself.

"Then why do you think it, dear sister?" Caleb demanded.

"Because I was told by someone, but I'm not sure who he was," Mary began.

And then she poured it all out at once. A torrent of words and tears and fears. The night Caleb came home so late and the visitor she had; the fear and confusion it had brought upon her; how she hadn't told anyone, especially Joseph; her plan to visit Elisabeth to confirm if what she had been told was true; the scripture Caleb had read in the synagogue and how she had run out terrified; about all her pondering on their journey here to Jerusalem, and whether she could ever return to Nazareth and that accursed door latch.

As she spoke, it was Caleb's turn to stare out the window as the light faded on the temple walls and the city became a dance of flickering lamps as if to reflect the stars which were just becoming visible in the clear night sky. Mary finished her story and restrained her sniffles as she waited for Caleb to speak. When he finally did, he didn't face Mary but continued to stare out the window.

"For probably the first time in my life," Caleb spoke slowly, "I have no idea what to tell you."

"For probably the first time in my life," Mary deliberately repeated, "I will tell you what to do."

Caleb turned from the window and Mary wondered if she had ever seen him cry, for now it looked as if he had.

"None of this makes any sense," Mary began. "If Elisabeth is not expecting, as I was told, if she is not, then I have been hallucinating or been troubled by evil spirits, or whatever."

Caleb shook his head and tried to interrupt her, but she cut him off.

"You must let me go see her, Caleb," Mary demanded. "I need to know. And if she is expecting, and in her sixth month as I was told, then," she paused to stifle another sniffle, "then I need time…time to see if I truly am expecting, because right now, I just don't know, Caleb."

"Mary," Caleb continued her thought, "You take all the time you need. Don't worry, I won't tell a soul."

"Yes you will." Mary corrected him. "If Elisabeth is expecting, and if I find out I am as well, then you will have to go and tell Joseph for me."

"Me? Are you sure that would be the right way to handle this?" Caleb questioned.

"I'm not sure of anything right now," Mary said, exasperated. "But I am sure that I could not bear to see his face when he finds out, if it is all true as I have been told."

"Perhaps you are right, Mary," Caleb resigned himself to her reasoning. "We are not sure of anything right now, so let's just go to sleep and tomorrow you go see Elisabeth."

"And within two Sabbaths as planned," Mary continued, "you come to visit Zechariah and Elisabeth and by then I will know."

Mary laid down on her sleeping mat as Caleb drew a blanket over the window.

"You do believe me, don't you Caleb?" Mary looked up expectantly.

"Of course I do. And whatever happens, we'll get through this together. You, me, even Joseph. You'll see."

"I hope so," Mary sighed deeply. "What would I ever do without you, Caleb?"

"Probably anything you wanted."

The laughter in his voice relaxed her and she finally closed her eyes, exhausted yet relieved for having shared her burden at last.

Caleb stooped to stroke her forehead as Mary whispered a prayer. He moved to the doorway but paused and decided to stay, watching over her as she fell asleep.

Chapter Nine
Elisabeth

Strange as the mat and home was to Mary, she slept soundly that night, having finally released at least some of the emotions that had been stirring in her heart for days.

The walk to Elisabeth's was only a three hour's journey and the road was travelled mostly by tradesmen and farmers from the surrounding hills of Judea, not like the more raucous and multi-national travellers on the routes north of Jerusalem. Caleb promised to come see her in two Sabbath's time and with a final hug that lasted longer than usual, he reassured her that everything was going to be all right.

"Are you sure you remember the way to go?" Caleb asked with that familiar tease in his voice that had been missing the night before.

"Of course I do. Just follow the main road west out of Jerusalem and within a few hours I will be nearing the town of Ain Karim."

"And Elisabeth's path will be opposite the rock pile on top of the second last hill before you reach the town," Caleb finished.

"It's the last hill," Mary corrected him.

"Second last hill," Caleb insisted. "I am the much travelled one, you know."

"And you are also the one who was so anxious to get to your

destination that you would scramble up the second last hill thinking it was a short cut to their farm, when actually following the path from the last hill was just as quick," Mary chided him.

"As long as you don't get lost," Caleb countered sheepishly.

"And if I did, which is highly unlikely," Mary assured him, "I would ask for directions."

"Fair enough," Caleb conceded, and he helped her arrange her basket of linens and clothing.

Carrying a few more fancy fabrics from Jerusalem that Jedediah's family had insisted she take, Mary started the final steps that she believed would answer the questions troubling her young heart.

The day was hot and sunny but with the descending hills the road to Ain Karim followed, breezes refreshed her at the rise of each, and the peaceful looking fields of grain and pastures calmed her spirit. How she used to love travelling this route with her parents as a child. And now she was travelling this route, possibly with child. How would this all work out? If she were to have a son, would she be able to give him the same secure childhood that her parents had given to Caleb and her? Would Joseph accept this child as his son and be a father to a child that was not his own? These and a thousand other thoughts robbed her of the beauty of the countryside and the courtesies of the simple people that passed her on the way.

Mary decided to rest for a short while as she reached the spot where the main road continued west and the lesser road turned south to Bethlehem. She had been to Bethlehem a few times with Elisabeth's husband Zechariah. As part of his priestly duties, it was Zechariah's job to check on the shepherds who tended the temple flocks of sheep on the hills outside Bethlehem. Thousands of lambs would be needed every year at the temple and Bethlehem sheep were known for their quality. Zechariah would go to Bethlehem to make arrangements for the delivery of the flocks to Jerusalem, especially at Passover.

On these journeys Mary and Caleb were thrilled to wander the hills with him, meeting with several groups of shepherds who all tried to extol the virtues of their flocks over all the others. Mary remembered how the young shepherds seemed more like boys than men, barely older than Caleb. Zechariah explained that boys and younger men made the best shepherds, being more fit to climb the hills, carry the lambs, and fight off predators. They could also stay out in the countryside for weeks without having to care for wives and children.

After this explanation, Zechariah would tell stories of their ancestors. His favourite stories were those of Bethlehem's most famous resident: the shepherd boy David who became the king of Israel. It was shepherding where he learned to sing psalms, to play the harp, to fight, and to trust God.

Mary was disturbed from her memories by a group of young shepherds rounding the corner from Bethlehem, bickering loudly as they tried to keep their small flock on the roadway.

Mary thought that perhaps that is where Caleb learned his marketing skills, watching the young shepherds bargain with the old priest. She gathered her thoughts and her burdens to finish the last hour of her journey.

Realizing she would soon arrive at Elisabeth's home, Mary began pondering how she would introduce the true purpose of her journey. Until that moment she had been preoccupied with getting there. She was sure they would both be home because if Zechariah was on duty in Jerusalem, they would have heard of it from

Zedediah. How could she inquire if Elisabeth was expecting without bringing any further shame on the aging, childless couple?

For the first time since deciding to visit Elisabeth to verify the visitor's prophecy over her, Mary began to doubt her plan. Maybe she had dreamed the whole episode, and even if it really happened, what if she had misunderstood the message about Elisabeth? If Elisabeth was not expecting than the whole incident must be her own imagination. Had the death of her parents actually messed up her mind? Her father always said she thought about things too much.

Lost in thought as she journeyed, Mary almost missed the turn onto the path at the rock pile. She considered forgetting about the whole thing, but decided not knowing would be worse than finding out that her mind had been playing tricks on her.

Once making the turn onto the northward path, she walked with a new resolve to complete her mission no matter what misunderstandings her visit may cause. At least she would be able to get back to Jerusalem quickly and save Caleb from sharing her embarrassment with Joseph.

Elisabeth's home came into sight and it was just as she remembered. A simple stone structure stood on a small rise of land facing the south where a view of the rooftops of Ain Karim could be seen. It was smaller than most farm homes since the lack of children had not forced Zechariah to build any sleeping rooms onto the main house. Elisabeth was an avid gardener and cultivated herbs and flowers around the house in addition to the grape vines that climbed on every available structure.

As Mary started up the stony path to the house, she could see Zechariah working outside. As she got closer, she called out to him. At first, it seemed he could not hear her, so she called out again. This time, Zechariah turned to see her, throwing his hands up in the air as he ran towards her.

Wildly waving his arms, he danced around her as he grabbed her bundles. Without saying a word, he beckoned her to the house and half dragged her with him. When they got to the door, he dropped her bundles and flung open the door. Then, waving his hands over his head again, he disappeared into the house. Mary had no idea why he didn't just call for Elisabeth to come. The old priest had always been a little eccentric, but this was strange behaviour, even for him.

Elisabeth appeared, looking the same to Mary as when she had cared for her when her mother died years ago. Mary stepped through the doorway as Elisabeth held out her arms to embrace.

"Shalom, Elisabeth," Mary began.

Before she could say anything else Elisabeth pulled away from her and grasping Mary by the shoulders she exclaimed in a voice loud enough to be heard in a marketplace:

"God's blessing is on you above all women, and his blessing is on the fruit of your womb. Who am I, that the mother of my Lord should visit me? I tell you, when your greeting sounded in my ears, the baby in my womb leapt for joy. How happy is she who has faith that Jehovah's promise will be kept!"

Mary had no time to process all that Elisabeth had just proclaimed, except that Elisabeth was indeed with child. And if she was, then what was told to her must be true. Unexpectedly, all the thoughts of her heart and all the Scriptures that her father had taught her poured out of her mouth. "Shout out, my soul, the greatness of the Lord. Rejoice, my spirit, in God my saviour; so tenderly has he looked upon his servant, humble as she is. For, from this day forth, all generations will call me blessed, so wonderfully has he dealt with me, the Lord, the Mighty One."

Zechariah continued to wave and dance around them as Mary emptied her heart. "His name is Holy, his mercy sure from generation to generation toward those who fear him; the deeds his own right arm has done display his might; the arrogant of heart and mind he has put to rout, but the humble have been lifted high. The hungry he has satisfied with good things, the rich sent empty away.

"He cheers on Israel his servant. Firm in his promise to our forefathers, he has not forgotten to show mercy to Abraham and his children's children, for ever."

With that, Mary collapsed into the arms of Zechariah, and the old priest half carried, half dragged her to a sleeping mat, without saying a word.

Chapter Ten
Confirmation

Mary woke to the sounds of Elisabeth arranging bowls on the kitchen table. She lay on a mat at the back of the house, unaware of when she had fallen asleep or how long she had been there. Rising, she felt stiffness in her legs from her days on the road. Refreshing herself with the bowl of water left by her bed, Mary brushed aside the curtain to see Elisabeth setting out the evening meal for Zechariah who reclined beside the table in silence. How old they looked in the dim light of the house, and to think that they were soon to be having a baby. And to think that Mary, as young as she was, would soon be having a baby as well.

"Well, you have decided not to sleep the whole day after all!" Elisabeth clucked at her as a hen would to her chicks as Mary stepped through the curtain.

"I'm sorry. I don't remember falling asleep, not even retiring to the mat," Mary apologized.

"Don't worry, child. You were so tired after your journey, you fairly collapsed into Zechariah's arms right at the door of the house. He carried you to your mat and you have slept through the rest of that day, all night, and most of this day. You must be hungry. Come and have something to eat."

"Thank you for taking care of me, Zechariah," Mary offered as she reached out her hand across the table. Zechariah looked at her with those knowing eyes of his but still said nothing as he reached across and grabbed her hand to give it a squeeze.

"Don't you go worrying about him, dear," Elisabeth volunteered as if to read the confusion on Mary's face. "He hasn't suffered any illness, and he's not just getting too old to speak. Although, he is getting old, and that's somewhat related to why he can't speak. Now let's start eating and I will tell you all about what has been happening to us. And then you shall tell us all that has been happening to you."

Elisabeth set down the bread and broth she had prepared and Zechariah was the first to dip his bread in the bowl and begin to eat. *If he can't speak, at least he can eat,* Mary thought as Zechariah became fully engaged with the meal and seemed to ignore the conversation that ensued.

"So you know," Elisabeth began, "that Zechariah and I were never able to have children. Not that we didn't want any, it just never happened, and as time went on we realized that it probably never would."

"You would have made such great parents," Mary tried to reassure her. "You were so good with Caleb and I when we would come to visit. We loved being with you!"

"And we loved having you, child. Maybe that's why we kept hoping for so long. Spending time with you kids kept us young and hopeful for a family of our own. It's one of the mysteries of life. Your parents fall asleep while you are still young and those of us with no children live longer than we deserve."

"But you are going to have a child at last, aren't you?" Mary pleaded as she began to fear she had misread the situation.

"Now hold on, dear, and let me give you the whole story," Elisabeth tried to calm her. "You remember that Zechariah as a priest would go to Jerusalem twice a year to take his turn at the temple."

"Yes, I know. We once met you there," Mary confirmed.

"That's right." Elisabeth said. "Remember Caleb took off on his own and we couldn't find him for two days?"

"I was younger and don't remember too much about it, except that my mother was crying the whole time!" Mary exclaimed. "If a child of mine ever did that I would surely die of worry!"

"Well, that brother of yours has been wandering off ever since. Where is he now, Mary?" Elisabeth inquired.

"He actually accompanied me as far as Jerusalem, and we stayed at Jedediah's house," Mary explained. "Before he heads back, he is going to come by to see you for a visit."

"And to take you back home with him?" Elisabeth concluded.

"I'm not sure about that," Mary voice faltered, for the first time looking away from Elisabeth's gaze. "I guess that becomes part of my own story."

"Well, dear, we have lots of time to talk about that later," Elisabeth reached out to stroke her arm. "Zechariah has been faithfully taking his turn at the temple all these years," Elisabeth continued. "And six months ago the lot fell upon him to offer the burnt incense in the holy chamber."

"Really?" Mary's voice regained its strength. "He must have been so excited!"

"Yes, excited and scared all at the same time. This privilege only comes once in a lifetime, and he was so nervous he wouldn't let me go with him to Jerusalem during that week," Elisabeth explained. "It was while he was there that he lost his voice."

"What happened?" Mary asked as she glanced at Zechariah who had finished eating and was joining the conversation by leaning forward with his mouth half open with a grin.

"Well, he was in the holy chamber, doing everything he was instructed to do." Elisabeth leaned forward as if not wanting to be overheard by anyone but Mary. "All of a sudden an angel appeared just to the right of the altar."

"What do you mean, an angel?" Mary cried out, surprising herself with the intensity of her words. "How did he know it was an angel?"

"There's no one else allowed in that chamber, dear," Elisabeth explained. "And it was an angel, of that there is no doubt!"

"Well, how could you know all this?" Mary was clearly agitated. "If Zechariah has lost his voice, how could you possibly know?"

Zechariah pushed a writing tablet towards her across the table until it was under Mary's hand.

"Your father taught you to read, did he not, Mary?" Elisabeth asked, as Mary nodded in reply. "Then read what the angel told Zechariah, just as he wrote it down once he returned home to me. Believe me, I was just as shocked as you seem to be now. It is both wonderful and fearsome all at once." Elisabeth wiped the beginning of a tear from her eye.

Mary took the tablet and began to read. The printing was small and cramped as if the writer was afraid he would run out of tablet before he ran out of words. Mary's hands trembled and she gasped as she read the words aloud.

"*Do not be afraid, Zechariah, for your prayer has been heard, and your wife Elisabeth will bear you a son, and you shall call his name John. And you will have joy and gladness, and many will rejoice at his birth, for he will be great before the Lord. And he must not drink wine or strong drink, and he will be filled with the Holy Spirit, even from him mother's womb. And he will turn many of the children of Israel to the Lord their God, and he will go before him in the spirit and power of Elijah, to turn the hearts of the fathers to the children, and the disobedient to the wisdom of the just, to prepare the people for the Lord."*

Mary looked up at Elisabeth and Zechariah, shaking as she remembered the words her own angel visitor had said to her.

Elisabeth reached forward to hold her shuttering hands and went on to explain. "Zechariah was so afraid, Mary. He didn't know what to say, but he dared to ask the angel how this could possibly happen, since he and I are old, far past the time for having children. Go ahead, dear, read on," Elisabeth encouraged her, as she gave her another tablet to read.

"I am Gabriel. I stand in the presence of God, and I was sent to speak to you and to bring you this good news. And behold, you will be silent and unable to speak until the day that these things take place, because you did not believe my words, which will be fulfilled in their time."

Mary could hardly finish reading, as she choked out the final words. The similarities between the angel that visited Zechariah and her were too much for her to comprehend. She looked up at Elisabeth from the tablet, crying as Zechariah reached for the tablet and held it to his chest as if he was reliving it all over again.

Elisabeth broke the silence as she continued the story. "When he left the chamber to come outside to bless the people, he couldn't speak. He used hand gestures and pointed at the objects around the temple to get them to understand that he had seen a vision. But he told no one what the angel had said to him until he came home to me. That was six months ago, and it wasn't long until I realized I was expecting. You can't imagine my joy, my confusion, my fear that at my age I would lose the child. So I hid myself and rarely went into town. I've told no one, and Zechariah, well, you can see that the angel said he would not be able to speak until the child is born, and surely he can't."

"And here I thought Zechariah was ill and suffering," Mary said, as she regained her composure.

"Oh, he's suffering all right. He has to listen to me all day long and can't get a word in," Elisabeth laughed. "Now tell me, Mary," Elisabeth leaned forward intently. "Did you know I was expecting? Is that why you came here? And how in the world did you find out when we haven't told a soul?"

"Me?" Mary exclaimed. "How did you know I was with child?"

"Why, I didn't!" Elisabeth objected. "Not until yesterday when you showed up to my door did the Spirit of Jehovah come over me. And it felt like the baby within me jumped for joy upon seeing you. At times I wondered if my baby was healthy because I hardly felt him move until that moment."

"I thought I saw you wince with pain," Mary admitted. "I was never so glad to see you in pain!"

"What is that supposed to mean, my dear?" Elisabeth questioned.

"Because then I knew you were with child and what the angel had told me about my own child was true and it would all come to pass," Mary admitted. She felt relieved that her secret was out and the purpose of her journey had been fulfilled.

"Whatever are you talking about, child?" Elisabeth asked, clearly confused.

"An angel came to me as well, Elisabeth!" Mary began, realizing for the first time she had admitted that the stranger who visited her must have been an angel. As soon as she said this, Zechariah jumped up from the table, returning with another tablet and began to write furiously. Mary tried to ignore him as she told Elisabeth all about the evening she had been alone, the visit from the angel, the amazing prophecy, the sign of Elisabeth being with child, her journey to their home, and her worries about Joseph and how her life would change forever in unpredictable ways.

Elisabeth listened intently, clucking ever so often in amazement. Zechariah had been busily writing on the tablet and as Mary finished her story he thrust it at her. On it he had written several questions about the angel Mary had seen. It was clear he wanted to compare notes on their experiences.

They talked late into the night, with Zechariah writing furiously about angel stories from the patriarchs to keep up with the conversation. After much laughter, tears, and wild gesturing from Zechariah, they finally retired to their mats, each to dream of all that was to come.

Chapter Eleven
Caleb Visits

The next two weeks passed quickly as Mary integrated herself into the life of Elisabeth and Zechariah. Simple household chores mixed with visits to the market kept Mary busy enough to not spend all her days pondering her situation. She helped Elisabeth prepare all the blankets and bedding and clothing they thought a new child would require. They laughed at the thought of the woman too old to give birth and a girl almost too young to give birth trying to help each other prepare for a birth. The blind leading the blind, they would say.

But they rejoiced often about the wonderful circumstances of the birth foretold to Zechariah, and worried just as often about the circumstances of Mary's pregnancy. For his part, Zechariah acquired more writing tablets and wrote down the prophetic greetings that Mary and Elisabeth had given each other, as best as either woman could remember them.

Elisabeth's secret was now out and all the townspeople knew that she was with child. Even as an older woman, her joy at having a child at last and the changes to her body made her appear a generation younger. Even Zechariah stepped a little lighter and stood a little taller, although his strange inability to speak was a constant source of amusement and bewilderment to the town.

Mary was glad that no one questioned why she was staying with them. Most assumed that as a young lady relative she was there to assist the older woman as the birth approached, and Mary said nothing to make them think differently.

As the time approached when Mary expected Caleb to arrive as they had arranged, she grew anxious. By then, it was clear to Mary that something was happening in her body, and she might very well be with child, as the angel said she would be. After all, the sign of the truth of the angel's prophecy was that Elisabeth was with child, and there was no doubt that she was. And Zechariah was convinced that the angel that visited him was the same that visited Mary. Everything in his study as a priest led him to believe so, and Mary had no reason to believe otherwise. It was all still as fearsome and wonderful as the day the angel visited her.

It was late afternoon while Mary gathered some overripe pomegranates that that she was startled by a voice behind her.

"Mary!"

For an instant, Mary thought Zechariah had miraculously regained his voice, when she realized who it was. "Caleb!" she cried, dropping her basket to throw her arms around him, releasing the tears that were always so close to the surface of her soul.

"Mary, have you not stopped crying yet?" Caleb teased.

"I have, but you just bring out the tears in me," Mary said, releasing her arms from around him to step back and study his face. "I'm so glad you're here, you won't believe all that has happened."

"I don't believe that I will," Caleb countered. "But I believe that you will find a way to convince me."

"You don't need me to convince you this time," Mary instructed him. "Just come see Elisabeth, full with child, just as the angel told me, and wait until you talk to Zechariah, well, you won't be able to talk with him, but you can talk to him, and—"

"Just slow down, my sister," Caleb cautioned her. "You're babbling on so fast you're not making any sense."

Mary dragged him back to the house where Zechariah greeted Caleb at the door with the wild gesturing that Mary was now quite used to. She saw the confusion on Caleb's face as he kissed his uncle on both cheeks. Elisabeth joined them at the door and got her guest to sit at the table while Zechariah went to fetch his tablets.

Elisabeth brought out the evening meal and so began another long evening of explaining to Caleb all that had happened and what it all might mean. When the conversation began to include what Mary should do next, they all decided to retire to their mats and leave that discussion for another day.

The next morning Caleb invited Mary to go for a walk among the hills as they had done so often as children. They clambered over the ancient stones and shuffled along the dusty paths until they came to an outcropping of rocks that afforded them a vista of the barren hills to the east and the Dead Sea in the far distance. Satisfied just to be with each other, neither said a word for the longest time, until Caleb broke the silence. "Then it must be true, as you were told," he began.

"It must be, Caleb!" Mary agreed. "My strange visitor must have been an angel. An angel told Zechariah that Elisabeth would be with child, told him he wouldn't be able to speak, and it all came true. The angel told me that Elisabeth would be with child, and she is."

"And the angel told you that you would bear a son," Caleb continued. "So that must be true as well."

Mary sighed deeply. "It must be."

"And, when will you know that you are?" Caleb asked awkwardly.

"I think I know already. Elisabeth and I have talked much and there is little doubt about it now," Mary said confidently. "I wish the angel had told me what I am supposed to do about it."

"That would have helped," Caleb agreed, standing up to stare off into the distance. "But you would think, if the angel knew all these things about you and Elisabeth and Zechariah, that he would have known that you were betrothed to Joseph, don't you think?"

"Would that have made a difference?" Mary was intrigued by his line of reasoning.

"For you to have a child on your own, especially a child of promise, would be a most difficult journey. But if you were married, then it would be no problem at all," Caleb reasoned.

"That's easy for you men to say," Mary argued. "We have to do all the carrying and birthing and feeding."

"I didn't mean it that way," Caleb apologized. "I meant it would be natural for a newly married couple to have a child, nothing unexpected at all."

Mary stood to her feet with a new resolve. "Then why not wait until I was married. Why now?"

"There must be a reason, we just don't know what it is," Caleb said. "But if your betrothal to Joseph goes ahead as planned in the next few months, then you will have a husband, and the child, and all will be well."

Mary was not so easily convinced. "And what if Joseph will not have me, knowing that I am with child?"

"Must he know?" Caleb asked.

"Of course he must know. We have never touched each other and in a few months it will be obvious I am with child. If he does not know the truth then he will assume the worst and double my shame!" Mary was indignant.

Caleb agreed quickly. "Yes, of course, he must know."

"And you shall tell him." Mary turned to face her brother. "We talked about this at Jedediah's, and I have not changed my mind."

"I am still not so sure." Caleb did not return Mary's stare.

"Well, I am." Mary refused to relent. "Now that we are sure all the angel said is going to happen, you will tell him as soon as you return to Nazareth."

"Then come with me back to Nazareth and you can be there as well to explain all that has happened to you and Elisabeth, and maybe he will then believe," Caleb argued.

It was Mary's turn to gaze off into the distance. "No, I have decided to stay with Elisabeth until she gives birth. She could use the help and I could use the education. That way, Joseph will have plenty of time to think things over and decide what he wants to do."

"And what do you wish him to do?" Caleb inquired.

"I wish that he would take me as his wife." Mary's voice shook. "But I will understand if he decides to put me away."

Caleb grasped Mary's face in his hands. "He would do no such thing, Mary. I know Joseph as well as I know any man, and he will do what is right."

"That is the problem, Caleb," Mary said. "None of us know what the right thing to do is. I even wonder if coming to see Elisabeth was the right thing to do."

"Of course it was. You had to know the truth about all that has happened to you," Caleb reassured her. "You must not be second guessing yourself all the time."

Caleb reached for Mary's hand and they began to pick their way down the stony path on their way back to Elisabeth's home.

"This evening begins the Sabbath, and the following day I will journey back home," Caleb offered. "I will only stay two days in Jerusalem, so I will be talking to Joseph before the next Sabbath. That will give him time to decide what to do before you return home. And time for me to negotiate."

"Negotiate?" Mary asked anxiously.

Caleb jumped across a small wadi in front of them as if he were a boy again. "Yes, that is what I am best at. Learned it all out here with Zechariah and the shepherd boys. There may be arrangements to be made, and compromises to consider. You must realize by now that you cannot have a normal wedding celebration, at least not in the condition you're going to be in."

Mary reached out her hand so Caleb could help her across the wadi. "You won't do anything I wouldn't approve of, will you?" Mary cautioned. "Joseph has been so good to me. I don't want you to hurt him."

"No one will be hurt. This will all work out, you'll see," Caleb reassured her. "Now let's get going. We don't dare be late for the Sabbath."

And with that, they continued in silence except for the occasional laughter at their difficulty in covering terrain that once presented no challenge to them.

Chapter Twelve

Confrontation

True to his word, Caleb bade farewell to the household of Elisabeth and Zechariah after the Sabbath, assuring Mary that he would have his talk with Joseph and get word back to her about his response. Elisabeth made him promise that he would share her news with Jedidiah so all the kinfolk in Jerusalem would know her barrenness had turned to blessing.

Caleb thought much about Mary's situation on his trip home, so much that he felt confident he missed out on some fine trading opportunities. The more he thought about it, the more he was convinced that if all this had come to pass as the angels foretold, surely the angels were aware of the situation between Joseph and Mary. After all, angels did the bidding of Jehovah, and everything Caleb knew of the Scriptures taught him that Jehovah knew the beginning from the end. It was impossible that Joseph did not fit into the scheme of things. With these thoughts in mind, Caleb resolved to talk to Joseph as soon as he arrived in Nazareth before his courage waned.

It was past time for the evening meal when Caleb arrived home. He fumbled with the latch on the door, forgetting how poorly it had been functioning of late. As soon as he put his travelling burdens down, he began the walk across town to Joseph's shop.

The last light of day cast long shadows as he arrived at the shop. He called out for Joseph but received no reply, so he opened the shop gate and stepped inside. Tools were laid about as if Joseph had left in the middle of a project, so Caleb decided to wait for his return.

As he went to close the gate, Joseph stepped through.

"Caleb! You gave me a fright! I never leave the shop gate open so I thought I was in for a confrontation." Joseph extended his arms to his old friend and they embraced in a hug. "I didn't expect you to be back with Mary for a couple more weeks!"

"Well, I am back, but not Mary." Caleb said. "She's going to stay with Elisabeth a while longer. They're really helping each other out. But I had to come back earlier. Business, you know." Caleb chose a stool to sit on. "I wanted to talk to you before tonight and thought I would wait for you here. Where have you been so late?"

"Just working on the land I want to build on for Mary. Nothing too exciting. Why did you want to see me?"

"It's Mary," Caleb offered as he shifted uncomfortably on the stool.

Joseph stepped toward Caleb. "What about Mary? Is she all right?"

"She's okay. There's just something she had to tell you and didn't know how. She asked me to do it before she came back home."

Joseph reached behind him and pulled the shop door shut. "Go on."

"I don't know how to tell you this, old friend." Caleb groped for a tool to fumble with as he spoke.

"It can't be all that bad, Caleb," Joseph tried to reassure him.

"It's not all that good, Joseph." Caleb tapped a chisel against his palm. "Mary is expecting."

"Expecting?" Joseph echoed. "Expecting what?"

"She's with child. She's going to have a baby."

"What? That's impossible!" Joseph raised his voice in defence. "I've never touched her! I would never!"

"I know, Joseph. It wasn't you." Caleb put the chisel back on the bench, relaxing now that the worst was over.

"Who, then?"

"I don't know, Joseph. I'm not even sure Mary does."

"How could she not know?" Joseph challenged. "Was she taken advantage of by someone? On that trip to Jerusalem! If she was, I swear I'll..."

Caleb cut him off before Joseph could utter anything rash. "It wasn't like that at all. During my last trip out of town, you remember, I was in Capernaum. She had a visitor after evening meal. He told her that she was going to give birth to a special child..."

"A special child? Sired by a special visitor, no doubt!"

Caleb rose to his sister's defence. "That's not how it was, Joseph. Mary said it was an angel who visited her."

Joseph laughed nervously. "Oh, now it's an angel story! That makes it okay! As long as an angel is involved then we must resign ourselves to the will of God! Who does she think she is? Another Sarah, or Hannah, or maybe the wife of Menorah? That's it! She's going to give birth to another Samson!" Joseph threw his hands up in the air.

"Don't mock," Caleb warned. "You know Mary as well as I do. She doesn't imagine things like some of the women around here. Something happened to her. I'm not even sure what, myself. She says she's going to have a baby and we have to believe her."

"I won't believe it unless I hear it from her myself." Joseph turned to open the shop door but Caleb quickly blocked his path.

"Not right now, you're not" Caleb used his larger size to his advantage. "That's why I came to tell you myself. So you'd have a chance to think about it and cool off before she comes home. You don't want to say anything rash that can spoil it for you two."

"Spoil it for us?" Joseph's voice trembled. "Don't you think having a baby that's not mine has spoiled things already?"

"Don't you think I know that? She was my sister before you were betrothed. We both care for her deeply," Caleb reasoned. "We have to trust her."

"To run away to Jerusalem," Joseph said.

"Of course not!" Caleb tried to sound reassuring.

"This whole story of going to see her cousin Elisabeth to supposedly prepare for our wedding..." Joseph shook his head in disbelief. "...and I fell for it."

"You didn't fall for anything, except to fall in love with Mary," Caleb corrected him. "And Elisabeth *is* helping her prepare for her wedding."

"And her child!" Joseph couldn't hide the hurt in his voice.

"Not just her child." Caleb searched for a way to convince Joseph. "This angel that visited Mary also told her that her cousin Elisabeth was in her sixth month."

"I thought she was barren," Joseph protested.

"We all did," Caleb confessed. "But Mary knew, because the angel told her. That is why she went to Elisabeth's, to see for herself. Everything the angel told Mary is true, so we must believe that Mary is telling the truth."

"So if she is telling the truth," Joseph countered, "Then she is going to have a baby that is not mine."

"Maybe not yours, but one that the angel said was being sent by

Jehovah." Caleb realized how fantastic it all seemed as he said it. "All I know is we need to trust her and see how it will all work out."

"I don't see how this can work out," Joseph said.

"Why don't we at least give it a chance?" Caleb pleaded. "She wants to stay with Elisabeth until she gives birth, to help her out. Then she'll come back home."

"You sure she wants to come back?" Joseph questioned.

"Of course she does! And now you have a little time to consider whether she will be coming back to you." Caleb's voice faltered. "Or not. This is more a problem for her than either of us. Let's at least wait until she comes home."

Joseph had been pacing the shop floor as Caleb pleaded with him. He approached Caleb and looked intently into his friend's eyes. "Only because you're my old friend would I ever agree to any of this." His voice softened.

"Only because of Mary," Caleb corrected him as he headed for the shop door. "Only for the love of Mary," Caleb repeated, and walked into the darkness.

Neither friend said goodbye; it had been a difficult conversation for both of them. Joseph closed the shop door and sank onto his work stool. *She deserves a chance*, he thought. But did he deserve to have to take a chance on her?

Chapter Thirteen

A Change of Heart

The sun beamed down and the hot day offered no breeze to discourage the flies from buzzing around Joseph's head. He straddled a roof beam as he chiseled away at the end to make a mortise. He had done this a dozen, perhaps hundreds of times before, but today he struggled. It had been two weeks since Caleb told him the news about Mary, and his frustration had increased with each passing day. He took little pleasure in his work, and his workmanship was suffering.

He had not even gone to the homesite he was clearing in preparation to build the house for Mary. Why bother continuing with his plan? Mary had left town, maybe never to return. She was with child, and the child was definitely not his, so maybe it was best if she never returned. And Caleb's story of angels and prophecies and Elisabeth's condition were all too fantastic to believe.

"I am a carpenter," Joseph said aloud, although he was alone and there was no one to hear. "I'm not a priest or a prophet. And I would have been happy to live my life and raise my family."

He swung himself off the beam to fit the tendon into the mortise, grunting in dismay as he realized he had not sufficiently trimmed the beam.

"Now I won't be happy doing anything." Joseph tugged at the beam to untether it. "I can't even trim a beam."

Finally releasing the tendon, Joseph set back to work chiseling. The energy for his work had left him, and he struggled through the day, tortured by thoughts of all his plans now laid waste. *Might as well leave Nazareth for good; there is nothing here for me now,* he thought. He could move north to Capernaum where the Romans were building a new administrative town. Work for a carpenter was easy to get, and the pay fair. He could save his money and start a new life somewhere, anywhere but Nazareth. He had lost his parents here, and now his betrothed. He should leave before he lost himself.

As the lowering sun indicated the end of the workday, it became clear to him what he had to do. He would sell the homesite back to the farmer from whom he bought it. The little bit of clearing and preparing of stones he had done would fairly compensate the farmer for his trouble. Then he would go to the elders at the local synagogue. Neither he, nor Mary, or Caleb had made it a secret that he had betrothed Mary. The whole village likely knew. There was no way to stop the marriage without the elders granting a writ of divorce. It wasn't done often, but when one party to the betrothal was caught in adultery, or somehow left town never to be seen again, it allowed the other party to cancel the betrothal without jeopardizing a future marriage.

Caleb, although he was young and much travelled, was rising in the ranks of leaders at the synagogue. Bringing shame upon him unnecessarily was not something Joseph wished to do. And since Mary had left town, no one knew about her condition. She could stay away, get married, and return if she wished with the child and no one would think anything out of the ordinary had happened. They would all assume that her family in Judea had arranged a marriage for her.

And what of me? he thought. What reason would he give the elders that he wished to cancel the betrothal? He couldn't tell them that Mary was with child; that would bring reproach upon her and her family. She had left town and not returned, at least not yet, and that would be reason enough. Or he could tell them that he had a change of heart, a change of plans, and could not ask a new wife to participate in them.

Many days he had worked this late preparing the site for their home, and walked back briskly full of energy for the next day. Today he was tired and discouraged, and didn't even bother to put his tools away.

Wanting to avoid conversation, he didn't bother having the evening meal with Obadiah's family, and instead retired to his mat in the shop. He lay awake for what seemed like hours, turning over in his mind all that had seemed so full of promise and all that had gone so terribly wrong. What could he have done differently? What great sin had he committed to have his heart broken?

Only the thought of seeing the elders gave him any peace. It was the only way out for all of them. He would still have to deal with Caleb, but at least it would be over for him and Mary. As he finally fell asleep, his last thoughts were wondering why his pillow was wet. Was it from sweating, or from tears?

Or was it from the rain? It wasn't even the rainy season, yet Joseph was standing in the rain, on a hillside that he did not recognize. It was not grassy and dotted with trees like the hills around Nazareth, but rocky with sparse patches of grass and shrubs. To his right he could just make out the rooftops of a town. Sheep huddled underneath a rocky outcrop on the hill opposite, with no shepherd in sight. The rain fell unrelenting, so Joseph sought shelter against a rocky ledge at his back. He wasn't sure what time of day it was, the skies being dark and foreboding.

How he got to this place and why, he did not know, but there was no use trying to make it to the town; he would have to wait for the rain to subside. He wondered why the shepherd abandoned his sheep in such a downpour. And then he saw him. The shepherd was walking amongst the sheep, checking on each one. Then he began to walk down the hill, leaving his sheep behind. Just as he dipped out of sight in the valley, Joseph realized the shepherd was walking up the hill towards him.

As he climbed the hill, Joseph noticed that this shepherd was dressed unlike any shepherd he had ever seen. He carried no staff or satchel, and his cloak was not the usual rough wool of his trade. It was longer, almost brushing the ground as he walked. It was a tightly woven knit of much finer material with long, full sleeves, more like a priest's robe than a shepherd's cloak. Now that he was close enough to see the shepherd's face, he looked older than most of the shepherds who stayed with the sheep in the hills. Usually they were boys, but this shepherd looked to be the same age as Joseph only he had no beard, which made his fine features all the more striking.

None of this frightened Joseph as he huddled against the rock in the rain. But when the shepherd came close enough to speak, Joseph was alarmed to see that the shepherd's cloak was not wet. The rain that soaked through Joseph's coat was not even landing on the shepherd's robe. Joseph looked down at the shepherd's bare feet—they too were dry, even though he had walked through the low shrubs and puddles to get up the hill. Joseph glanced to his right to make sure there was a town nearby and thought that maybe now he would make a run for it.

"Joseph!" The shepherd's voice was deep and steady, and it seemed to echo against the rock behind Joseph. Joseph's eyes left the town and his way of escape to fix upon the face of the shepherd. His eyes were dark, deep pools of blackness that seemed to reflect everything around them.

Joseph, sensing he was trapped, responded. "How do you know who I am? Who are you?"

"Joseph, son of David," the shepherd ignored his question. "Do not fear to take Mary as your wife, for that which is conceived in her is from the Holy Spirit."

This frightened Joseph. Not only did this shepherd know who he was, he knew about Mary and her pregnancy. And he knew about his reluctance to continue with their betrothal. Caleb must have told him, and maybe others. Soon everyone would know. But what does it mean that it is from the Holy Spirit? How is that possible? Joseph had no time to contemplate before the man spoke again.

"She will bear a son, and you shall call his name Yeshua." The shepherd's voice was now both echoing and booming in Joseph's ears so he could not tell if the shepherd had spoken once or a dozen times.

Struggling to comprehend, Joseph repeated the prophecy. "Mary will have a son, and I am to call him Yeshua? No one in my family has ever had that name," Joseph protested, overwhelmed.

"You shall call his name Yeshua, for he will save his people from their sins," the shepherd confirmed Joseph's question.

"He will what?" Joseph was more frightened now than ever. But the shepherd had turned away from Joseph and began to walk down the hillside.

Joseph sprang from the shelter of his rocky ledge to follow, so many questions he needed answered. But as he stepped out into the driving rain, he saw that the spot where the shepherd stood was dry. All around the heavy rain had begun to puddle and little rivulets drained down the hillside, but where the shepherd had stood remained dry. As Joseph stared after him in amazement, he could see in the shadowy light that everywhere the shepherd walked was dry, as if his feet were sponges, instantly soaking up the water.

The shepherd disappeared in the valley, and as he began his climb up the other hillside, a little lamb, apparently escaping from the flock, climbed out of the valley, bounding up the hill towards Joseph, slipping and stumbling on the soggy ground. The shepherd made no attempt to retrieve his lamb, but kept climbing the hill towards the flock.

Bleating as it ran, the lamb came straight towards Joseph. He bent down to grab it before it ran past him. Joseph nearly lost his grip on the soggy wool but managed to hold on. As he cradled it in his arms, he looked up to see if the shepherd was coming to retrieve the lamb, but the shepherd and his flock were nowhere in sight.

Reaching for his coat to shelter himself and the lamb better from the rain, Joseph realized that his coat was dry. The driving rain was not making him wet at all. He felt his hair and his beard and they were dry. He stood up in disbelief, cradling the lamb in his arms. Returning to the shelter of the rock, he collapsed in a heap of emotion, sobbing uncontrollably as the lamb snuggled into the crotch of his elbow, falling fast asleep.

Chapter Fourteen

His Name is John

Hardly a day went by without a woman from the village stopping in to see Elisabeth. Mary couldn't remember the names of everyone she met in the two months she had stayed with Elisabeth. As word got around that Elisabeth was finally to be blessed with a child, they would stop by to congratulate her. With them they brought clothing for her and baskets of leftovers from their own child-rearing days. Elisabeth graciously accepted all offerings.

Less graciously accepted was all the advice and supposed wisdom that never ceased to flow from the mouths of the mothers who had walked this path before. Warnings about the difficulties of labour, how they could tell whether the baby would be a boy or a girl, the many pitfalls of child rearing; there was no topic they did not have an opinion about. Mary listened dutifully and nodded her head in agreement whether she valued their tales or not.

She didn't dare join in the conversations lest she inadvertently reveal her own pregnancy. By now her body was swelling as it should and she was careful to always wear loose fitting garments. Elisabeth had no problem agreeing to keep her secret, since she herself had hidden her pregnancy for five months. Mary had been one of the first to know, other than Zechariah, who of course wasn't saying a word. She was worried that she hadn't heard from Caleb yet, so she had no idea if he had spoken to Joseph or not, and if he had, what Joseph's reaction had been.

She was so busy with Elisabeth's childbirth she had little time to ponder her own situation. Zechariah had set up a tent past the garden for Elisabeth to give birth in. Whether it was because he was a priest and liked to do things the traditional way, or because he was mute and couldn't bear all the chatter from the women in the house, Mary wasn't sure. But Mary managed the house and meals, while Elisabeth laboured in her tent with her midwife and far too many other women than necessary.

On the morning of the third day in the tent, Mary was still putting out the morning meal for Zechariah when one of the women came to the door. Elisabeth was about to give birth, and was asking for Mary.

Zechariah reached across the table and squeezed Mary's hand, looking steadily into her eyes. Mary had lived with him long enough to know this was his way of calming her, of letting her know that just as Elisabeth's childbirth was coming to pass, so too would hers. Many times over the past months he had calmed her in just such a manner. Sometimes he would get his writing tablet and write down words of the Scriptures for her to read. Elisabeth had helped her understand the ways of childbirth, but it was the mute old priest who had helped her understand the ways of Jehovah.

Mary hurried out to the tent, not sure what to expect. She found Elisabeth crouched over with a woman on either side supporting her arms and back. Another had spread a fresh blanket on the ground in front of her and had a pan of water to the side. Between her groans,

Elisabeth looked up at Mary and gave her a weak smile. Mary tried to smile back, but could only manage a look of sympathy for the pain she must be in, especially at her age.

Between deep breaths Elisabeth managed to say: "He who is mighty has done great things for me."

Mary recognized this as what she had prophesied all those months ago when she arrived at Elisabeth's door. Conscious of the other women in the tent, Mary said nothing but came behind her so she could squeeze Elisabeth's hand. Elisabeth squeezed her hand in return and began another bout of groans. Mary tried to release Elisabeth's grasp but Elisabeth squeezed all the harder. This time the groaning ended with a cry as Elisabeth pushed for the final time. The midwife caught the baby before it reached the blanket and Mary felt Elisabeth's grasp loosen. The women beside her eased Elisabeth onto her back so she was laying down. Mary dampened a cloth and sat beside her, wiping her forehead and whispering prayers as the midwife cleansed the baby.

"You have a man child!" the midwife finally exclaimed as she wrapped the baby in the swaddling clothes Elisabeth had prepared.

"There was never any doubt!" Elisabeth replied as she reached for Mary's hand.

Mary held her hand and spoke softly so only Elisabeth could hear. "And blessed is she who believed that there would be a fulfillment of what was spoken to her from the Lord."

Elisabeth laughed, recognizing her own greeting to Mary was now being applied to her. The midwife brought the baby to Elisabeth and she snuggled it to her bosom.

"Go tell Zechariah," Elisabeth told Mary. "Go tell him what he already knows."

Mary did as she was bidden and went back to the house. Zechariah was standing in the doorway, and before Mary could speak he was already spreading out his arms to embrace her.

"You have a son!" Mary's well of emotions burst and she began to cry.

Zechariah laughed as he held Mary in his embrace; a laughter of relief and gladness. As the old priest laughed, Mary sobbed as she realized all that had come to pass for Elisabeth would soon happen to her, and she would have no laughing priest to be there for her. She may be all alone. But Zechariah's laughter soon turned to tears of joy, and Mary was relieved to think he might mistake her tears for joy as well. They stood in the doorway for minutes, the old priest and the young lady crying in each other's arms.

The celebration of the birth lasted for days. The midwife and the other women spread the news of the birth of the child, and there was a never ending procession of relatives and neighbours coming to the house. Elisabeth decided to stay in the tent until the boy was circumcised on the eighth day. That way Mary and Zechariah could entertain their guests at the house, many of whom travelled more than a day's journey and needed to stay the night. Mary was kept so busy keeping up the gardening, cooking, and arranging sleeping quarters that she had little time to think of her own situation and plan to return to Nazareth. No news had come from Caleb and Mary was beginning to think it didn't matter. Whatever news Caleb could bring, there was no good way for her situation to work out.

Elisabeth mothered as if she had been doing it all her life. Mary hoped that nursing and caring for a baby came as natural to her as it did to Elisabeth. On the morning of the eighth day, more than a dozen relatives from as far away as Jerusalem and Hebron came for the celebration of circumcision. As a priest, Zechariah had done this dozens of times, and had a whole ceremony planned. Only this time, he would not be able to do any of the readings from the Law that accompanied the ritual.

Everyone thought Zechariah had lost his voice due to illness or a judgment from Jehovah for breaking some part of his priestly vow. Mary and Elisabeth would not comment otherwise. They thought Zechariah had written on the tablet that the angel had said he would not be able to speak until the child was born. But the birth had not changed his condition, so Mary and Elisabeth were no longer sure what to think.

The whole ritual took less than half an hour. A relative who was a priest from Hebron did the readings from the law. He did so as Zechariah did the cut, so the little baby's cries were mingled with the cry of the Law of Jehovah. As the men gave the boy back to Elisabeth, they made the official announcement of the boy's name: Zechariah.

As the firstborn boy, and likely to be the only child as everyone assumed, he should be named after his father Zechariah. That name had been carried on in the family for generations, as long as anyone could remember.

It was Elisabeth's voice who silenced the group. "No. He shall be called John."

No one knew what to say. It was the man's job to name the child. Women did not have a say, at least not publicly.

Zedidiah spoke up first. "None of your relatives is called by this name," he said in a tone of accusation. The gathering of relatives and neighbours all agreed, but Elisabeth stood her ground. They began, as best they could, to motion to Zechariah to see what his response to

Elisabeth would be. After these months, Mary knew when Zechariah wanted his writing tablet, and as he motioned in her direction, she quickly got the one that he kept by his mat.

Zechariah grasped the quill that Mary offered him and wrote in a steady hand: *His name is John.*

Murmurs of dissent amongst the gathering grew into loud objections and questions as to why this name should be appropriate.

One voice rose above the others and none were more surprised than Mary and Elisabeth that it was the voice of Zechariah:

"Blessed be the Lord God of Israel, for he has visited and redeemed his people and has raised up a horn of salvation for us in the house of his servant David."

Zechariah voice was loud and clear. Months of silence and pondering and searching the Scriptures to unlock the mysteries that the angel had told him now tumbled out of the old priest's heart and into the ears of his assembled guests.

"As he spoke by the mouth of his holy prophets from of old, that we should be saved from our enemies and from the hand of all who hate us. To show the mercy promised to our fathers and to remember his holy covenant, the oath that he swore to our father Abraham. To grant us that we, being delivered from the hand of our enemies, might serve him without fear, in holiness and righteousness before him all our days."

No one dared to move or speak. It was as if the priest was caught up in another realm. The words flowed so effortlessly it was like he was reading them from a scroll. He walked over to Elisabeth and took the boy from her, continuing his prophecy.

"And you, child, will be called the prophet of the Most High, for you will go before the Lord to prepare his ways, to give knowledge of salvation to his people. In the forgiveness of their sins, because of the tender mercy of our God, whereby the sunrise shall visit us from on high to give light to those who sit in darkness and in the shadow of death, to guide our feet into the way of peace."

Zechariah kissed his son before giving him back to a weeping Elisabeth. The women gathered around her, while the men helped Zechariah, now exhausted, enter the house to sit at the table.

Mary could scarcely keep her composure. Everything the angel had told Zechariah had come to pass; he was able to speak again. And what a speech! All these prophecies from Elisabeth, Zechariah, and even herself were overwhelming. What did they all mean, and was it possible that they were all involved in a great plan that none of them completely understood? The angel had told her that her child would be the Son of the Most High and sit on the throne of David. And Elisabeth had greeted her as the mother of her Lord; how could she forget that? And now Zechariah spoke about the house of David and how this child would be a prophet of the Most High.

It was all too monumental for her to understand. There was no one who could help her understand. Maybe once the crowds had left in a day or so she would be able to talk to Elisabeth and Zechariah alone and sort all of this out. She was interrupted from her thoughts by a hand on her shoulder. It was Zedidiah from Jerusalem.

"How are you, Mary? Are you well?" His voice was kind.

"Yes, just overwhelmed by all that has happened here," Mary confessed.

"We all are. These are most unusual events for our family. What will become of this child, with all of this happening?" Jedidiah wondered out loud.

Mary did not dare to answer, so she said nothing.

Jedidiah did not seem aware of her silence, and continued. "Caleb has sent word for you, Mary. He sent a gift by caravan for me to bring to Elisabeth, and with it a message that you were to come home as soon as you were able. He knew you were planning to stay with Elisabeth until she gave birth, and now he wants you to come home to Nazareth."

"Come home?" Mary was afraid the fear was evident in the tone of her voice.

"Why, yes," Jedidiah confirmed. "He misses you terribly. He doesn't eat properly when you are not there to go to market. And Caleb says a certain young man, Joseph as I recall, awaits your return as well." Jedidiah's eyes brightened and his voice betrayed his teasing.

Mary tried to hide the tension in her voice. "Joseph?"

"I'm sure that was his name. A young carpenter by trade, a pretty good one, at that." Jedidiah was still teasing her. "He is the one who made the gift Caleb sent for Elisabeth. The message said the gift was from all Elisabeth's family in Nazareth, whoever they might be. Did you not see it?"

"I'm sorry, I've been so busy managing the household, I haven't," Mary told truthfully. "What did Caleb send?" Mary chose her words carefully.

"I'll show you," Jedidiah offered, and walked over to the small cart he had dragged along with his family's provisions. He returned with a basket, shaped like the baskets that newborns would lie in. Only the basket was not made of reeds, but wood. Different colours of wood were shaved thin and weaved intricately with all the sharp edges sanded smooth and oiled until it shone.

"Apparently it's the first one he's ever made, and a fine one it is," Jedidiah bragged to Mary as he gave it to her and rejoined the men. Rubbing the polished sides of the basket, she hurried away from the others until she was alone. Squatting on the ground she cradled the basket in her lap and began to weep.

Chapter Fifteen

The Road Home

It was time for Mary to return home. All the excitement surrounding the birth and naming of John had passed. The tent had been dismantled and Mary had the garden and baking and a dozen other household duties in good order. Now that Zechariah was talking again, the news of their circumstance had spread throughout the hill country of Judea. Every day someone stopped at the house to hear the story firsthand. And every day Mary and Elisabeth wished for at least one more day of silence from the priest.

Elisabeth was as good a mother as any young mother would be. She had no need of a nursemaid, and Mary was sure her neighbours would continue the help that she had been providing around the house. They had talked about what Mary should expect when she returned to Nazareth and all the challenges she may face. Elisabeth reminded Mary that just as the angel's prophecies came true for them, so she would have to give the angel's prophecy time to come true for her.

Mary prepared for the journey back to Nazareth. She was leaving with more than she brought, having sewn several blankets and garments that she would soon need to wear. It had been three months since the angel's visit and if Mary wore the same clothes now that she came with to Elisabeth's, it would be obvious to anyone she was with child.

As she said farewell to baby John, she stroked the basket Caleb sent. Whatever possessed him to send such a gift, and however he convinced Joseph to make it, she did not know. But these and a hundred other questions that had plagued her heart would never be answered if she did not return home.

The morning of her leaving was clear. A gentle breeze beckoned her along the path. She would make the day's journey to Jerusalem and stay with Zedidiah. She would then join the next group of pilgrims heading up the Jordan Valley northward. It was festival season so there would be travellers leaving from the temple in Jerusalem and Mary would be safe among them.

"The Lord bless you and keep you, my child," Elisabeth hugged her for the final time.

"The Most High works in mysterious ways," Zechariah said. "You have seen that here, no doubt."

"Mysterious and often troubling ways," Mary agreed.

"Whatever may happen in Nazareth, you are always welcome here. The house of Zechariah is your home as well," Zechariah offered.

Mary bowed her head in thanks to the priest, who held her by the shoulders and looked intently into her eyes when she raised her gaze again. He reached for a parchment and pressed it into her hand. Mary opened it long enough to see it was the writings he had made on the tablets when he could not speak: the greetings that Mary and Elisabeth had shared, his encounter with the angel, and the events surrounding baby John's circumcision. Mary closed it and held it tightly to her chest.

"To remind you of all that the Lord has done," Zechariah instructed.

"I will treasure these days in my heart always," Mary assured them. She started on her way, pausing at the well to look back at her aging cousins. They waved her on, and Mary continued down the path, not knowing when she would return to this house of miracles.

The walk to Jerusalem was uneventful, but Mary realized how tired she was once she reached Jedidiah's in time for the evening meal. She certainly could not travel as easily as she had three months before.

It had been only a few days since the circumcision celebration, so there was not much news to share. Mary only had to endure a little more teasing from Jedidiah about the carpenter from Nazareth before she was able to retire to her mat.

Sleep, however, eluded her. She had not slept well when staying here on her way to Elisabeth's, her heart so troubled by the angel's visit; and now, despite all the amazing events at Elisabeth's, her heart was still troubled by what would happen to her now that she was with child and alone. Eventually she fell asleep, but seemed to be wakened immediately by Jedidiah calling for her. He had been to the temple early and there was a caravan leaving at the third hour. If she hurried, she could join them.

She was annoyed by having to leave in a rush, but grateful to not have to stay and make small talk over a morning meal. Mornings were the worst for Mary as she often felt sick if she ate, and did not always keep food down. She washed quickly and grabbed her belongings. Jedidiah went with her to catch the caravan, which held a mix of pilgrims from the temple and tradesmen heading north to seek work. Jedidiah talked to some of them to make sure they would watch out for Mary as she was travelling alone, and then he kissed her goodbye.

It was three day's journey back to Nazareth, and it was three days for Mary to rehearse all the scenarios she might encounter once she arrived home. Lost in her thoughts, she engaged in little conversation with the other women, other than what was needed to arrange meals and sleeping arrangements. The days were long, as the men were anxious to keep moving. Mary was exhausted and her back and feet ached by the end of the day. Thankfully she was so tired that sleep came quickly once she was on her mat. By the middle of the third day, the part of the group going through Nazareth broke off from the main caravan and left the valley road to climb the green hills heading west.

By the ninth hour of the day, they reached the village and Mary said her thanks and farewells before starting down the familiar streets to her house. It was much too early for Caleb to be home, even if he was doing his trading locally. Mary was relieved to think she would have time to think before having to talk to Caleb about all that had happened at Elisabeth's.

The streets were quiet and no one seemed to notice Mary as she made her way home. Reaching the house, she put down her baskets and reached for the door. Ever since the angel's visit the latch had played with her mind and brought back all the turmoil of that night. Sighing as she prepared herself to fight back the emotions stirring within her again, she pulled on the latch, but it had been changed. The old latch was gone and in its place was a sturdier one, much like the ones she had seen on the shops in Jerusalem.

Both pleased and perplexed, Mary entered her home. Everything was as she had left it, only showing evidence that a man had been living here alone without a woman to keep house. The shelf for the casks of oil and cooking supplies was nearly bare and the table was littered with dirty cups and oil lamps that hadn't been trimmed. The floor looked like it had not been swept since she left, and as she pulled back the curtain to look at the sleeping mats, the blankets and pillows were in disarray. Robes were piled in the corner.

"Men!" Mary said aloud. She retrieved her baskets from the door and put them by the table. She trimmed a lamp and lit it to make her feel more at home. Too tired to clean the house, she found a basin with a little bit of water left in it and washed her feet. She tidied the area around one of the sleeping mats and laid down. She fell asleep at once, although a fitful sleep where she was aware of the passage of time.

Caleb noticed the glow of the lamp through the window of the house when he turned the corner to head up the street to their home. *Mary must finally be home,* he thought, *and not a day too soon.* Joseph had been asking for her every day he saw Caleb, and the days their paths didn't cross, Joseph sought him out to ask him yet again when Mary would be home. He had already seen Joseph that day and told him there was no news yet, so Caleb was sure Joseph would not show up at the house tonight. He would get the chance he needed to talk to Mary first.

"Mary?" It was Caleb kneeling by her mat. "Are you awake?"

"I am now, thanks to my considerate brother," Mary scolded him lovingly.

"I brought some bread and fish from the market for a meal," he offered. "Why don't you join me and we can talk while we eat?"

Mary propped herself up on an elbow. "Did you think to bring any fresh water?"

"Who, me? A grown man carrying a water pot?" Caleb grinned at her, and stepped beyond the curtain. Before Mary was off her mat, he reappeared with a jug of water, still showing off his boyish grin. After Mary had washed her face, she joined him at the table which he had hastily cleaned off.

They sat at the table and did more talking than eating. Mary reminded him about what he already knew from his visit to Elisabeth's and told him all about the birth of John, at least the parts that a man would take interest in. He listened intently as she told him about the circumcision and how Zechariah got his voice back, and hadn't stopped talking since; about Jedidiah teasing her about the carpenter from Nazareth and how she tried to ignore him.

"So your journey was a success, then," Caleb offered

Mary was finally able to unburden all the wondering and pondering she had done on her journey back home. "If you mean, did I confirm that what the angel told me?" Mary began.

Caleb interrupted her. "Angel? You would only say it was a strange visitor. Now you are sure it was an angel?"

"There is no doubt about it, Caleb," Mary rose to his challenge. "After talking with Zechariah about his encounter with an angel in the holy temple, I have no doubt that my visitor was an angel."

"Why, though? What does it all mean?" Caleb questioned.

"I'm still trying to figure it out," Mary admitted. "But everything the angel told me about Elisabeth came true, and everything the angel told Zechariah came true." She paused to position herself more comfortably at the table. "And everything the angel told me is coming true. There is no doubt, Caleb. You are going to be an uncle to a baby boy in about six month's time." Mary said with a confidence in her voice that even surprised her.

Caleb rose from the table, shaking his head; whether in disbelief or amazement, Mary could not tell. He walked over to the doorway as if to leave.

"You believe me, don't you, Caleb?" Mary was unsure of his response. "This child I am carrying is not a result of a fault I have committed. It is a child of God, whatever that may mean!"

"Of course I believe you!" Caleb protested. "Of all the people in Nazareth I would be the one to believe you, even if no one else did. And a boy!" Caleb's eyes brightened and Mary sensed excitement in his voice for the first time.

"For sure," Mary confirmed. "It will be a boy."

Caleb was still standing at the doorway, when Mary thought about the new latch.

"When did you put a new latch on the door?" Mary asked.

"Oh, that," Caleb answered. "That old latch was never working right since you left for Judea. I got so tired of it I bought a sturdier one in Jerusalem and got Joseph to install it."

"Joseph!" Mary sighed. "You must tell me what you have told him." Mary's voice was firm. "You did not send word while I was at Elisabeth's, and you have conveniently avoided telling me now."

"I have not avoided it, Mary," Caleb protested. "You have been doing most of the talking, and I have been waiting for the right time."

"That time has come," Mary instructed him. "I have had enough sleepless nights wondering what he will think of me. I will not sleep another night until I know."

"The first thing you must know is I talked to Joseph as soon as I returned from seeing you at Elisabeth's," Caleb began. "I met Joseph at his shop and told him you were with child and it was not because you had been with any man."

"And he believed you?" Mary asked anxiously.

"He didn't know what to think, Mary." Caleb explained as he sat down again at the table and poured himself another cup of wine. "At the time, I didn't know what to think."

"What did he say?" Mary tried to hold back the tears that were always close to the surface whenever she talked to Caleb about these matters.

"He thought that maybe you went away to Elisabeth's, not to prepare for your wedding, but to escape and never return," Caleb said, noticing Mary's head dropping to her chest. He reached over and lifted her face with his hands so he could look her in the eyes. "But he decided—we decided—that we would do nothing, and say nothing, until you returned from Judea," Caleb said as sincerely as he could. "We were waiting for you, Mary. It will be your baby, and we both care about you more than anything."

"I'm not so sure about that," Mary admitted. "I mean, I know you care about me, Caleb. You have to. I am your sister. But Joseph?" Mary looked away from Caleb. "He would have every right to put me away."

"I don't think he will, Mary," Caleb said.

"Did he say so?" Mary challenged him.

"No, not in so many words," Caleb admitted. "We didn't talk about it again for some time. There was nothing new to talk about. I told him that Elisabeth was with child, and that somehow you knew. About a week later, he brought this baby basket that he had made and asked me to make sure it got to Elisabeth."

"You mean you didn't ask him to make it?" Mary's voice broke as she fought the emotions welling up inside her.

"No! I had no idea what he was doing!" Caleb shrugged. "I didn't even know that we were supposed to sent gifts for a baby."

"Of course you wouldn't!" Mary agreed.

"But somehow Joseph did," Caleb admitted. "And when he gave it to me, he said that it was a gift for you as well."

"For me?" Mary rose from the table to try and hide the tears she could no longer hold back.

"Well, not for you. He said it was for Elisabeth's baby, but you would know what it meant," Caleb explained as he got up to hold Mary as she cried softly. "Crying again, dear sister?" Caleb said kindly. "All I ever do is make you cry!"

Chapter Sixteen

Her Fears Are Gone

Mary had been home for three days before Caleb talked to her about arranging a time for her to meet with Joseph. She was so tired from her visit with Elisabeth and her journey home that Caleb wanted her to catch up on her rest. Even he could notice her body and face were changing, and household activities tired her more than before. He had told Joseph that Mary was now home, but needed time to rest up and refresh herself before they met to talk about the betrothal.

Caleb tried to get Joseph to tell him what his intentions were, but Joseph would say nothing. He said he wanted to talk to Mary first, and Caleb would find out soon enough, but his continual questions about how Mary was doing was a hopeful sign. Caleb wanted it to all work out for them, whatever that meant. As the older brother in charge of his sister's affairs, he could force his will upon her, but all the talk of angels and prophecies made him hesitate.

For her part, Mary busied herself getting the house back in order. On her trips to the market and well, all who knew her were glad to see her return. They asked about Elisabeth's baby and Mary told them all they needed to know. She didn't tell them about her own involvement in all that had happened, and everyone assumed that she was there to assist the older woman, and that was true enough. Mary was glad to wear the new clothes she had made at Elisabeth's, as they hid her condition. Any plumpness in her facial features were the mark of a girl maturing into a woman.

It was the day Sabbath began at sunset that Caleb arranged for Joseph to meet Mary and go for a long walk together. Mary wondered why he would choose this day when she had to make all the preparations for the Sabbath. Because, Caleb reasoned, Mary would have to be back home by sunset, so there would be a definite end to the conversation, however it went. There would be no opportunity for it to drag on and on with no benefit to either of them.

"Are you sure, Caleb?" Mary asked him the night before the day of the meeting.

"Quite sure, dear sister," Caleb assured her. "When I want to make a sale or a trade, I don't give my customer all the time in the world to consider. I give him a block of time in which to negotiate and that is all."

"I don't think this should be a sales job," Mary objected.

"No. But you are trying to make a decision about how you two should continue your lives," Caleb reminded her. "Joseph has had two months to think it over. It is time you knew his intentions so you can plan your life accordingly. Delaying any longer will do no good for any of us."

And so it was that Mary rose early the day of the Sabbath and began her chores. The house needed to be swept clean. The special garments they set aside for wearing to the synagogue were brushed and laid out. All the lamps were filled with oil. She went to the well and filled the water jugs. Going to the market, she purchased some bread, oil, and herbs with money that Caleb left for her. At home she prepared the evening meal, and another meal for the Sabbath day.

It was past the sixth hour when Mary finally finished the essentials she had to do. She would have busied herself for the whole day, in a nervous attempt to avoid the inevitable, but thought better of it and went to wash her face. She removed the tunic she wore for doing housework and put on one of the dresses she had made at Elisabeth's. As she arranged her hair underneath her hood she heard a knock at the door. Joseph must have left work at noon to come for her, and for a moment she panicked; but the time had come for her to face her fears, and with a steady hand she opened the door.

Joseph stood before her, appearing taller than Mary remembered. He wore his best robe, the one with the long sleeves he would normally wear to the synagogue. His beard was trimmed and his eyes were bright with kindness. He reached out his hand and touched the sleeve of her gown.

"Mary!" Joseph could not hide the excitement in his voice at the sight of her.

Mary could not speak. It was so good to see his chiselled face and rough hands again. She had spent months with priests and gardeners and city folk from Jerusalem and she had forgotten how handsome Joseph was and how safe she felt when she was near this strong and rugged man.

She started to close the door, indicating to him that they would speak outside. Joseph obliged, and Mary shut the door and fixed the latch before finally finding the courage to speak. "Thank you for fixing the door latch," she said meekly.

"It was nothing," Joseph shrugged. "Caleb brought one from Jerusalem. The house was falling apart without you."

Mary nodded, but kept looking down the street, afraid of the emotions that might erupt if she looked at him.

"And so was I," Joseph informed her.

"You were?" Mary asked. She had been trying to guess what Joseph was thinking, but now he left no doubt.

"Yes, I was. More than you could know," Joseph continued. "I was okay with you going to Elisabeth's to visit and prepare for the wedding. That was no problem. When Caleb returned a few weeks later and told me that," Joseph hesitated to say what they both knew he meant. "Well, you know what he told me." Joseph avoided saying it out loud.

Mary said nothing as they walked down the street.

"I will admit, I was confused," he said. "I thought maybe someone had taken advantage of you; maybe you had tricked me; maybe our betrothal was too hasty; maybe it was over between us." Joseph stopped to look at her. "I thought maybe you were never coming back, and that was the worst thought of all."

Mary returned his gaze and could see the kindness in his face. He wasn't angry or even hurt. He only looked like he had lost something very valuable to him and was now searching to find it.

"I always intended to come back," Mary finally replied. "It just seemed the right thing to do, to stay until Elisabeth had her child." How she wanted to tell him about how the angel's prophecy had been confirmed and all the amazing events in Judea, but she didn't want to force his decision. She wanted to hear what he really thought without all the events of her life making the decision for him.

"I'm so glad you did," Joseph smiled at her while they continued walking. "And then I had a dream," Joseph said tentatively. He had told no one about his dream, not the family he was staying with, not with Caleb. He wanted Mary to be the first to hear about it, and maybe the last. But now that he was speaking it out loud it sounded fantastic even to him.

"A dream?" Mary exclaimed with excitement in her voice. "What do you mean, a dream?"

"I mean a dream," Joseph confirmed. "Don't you remember our patriarch Joseph had dreams? I am his namesake, and so I, too, had a dream."

"Go on," Mary encouraged him.

"I dreamt that I was on a hillside in the pouring rain. On the hill opposite me was a flock of sheep and a shepherd. The shepherd left his flock and crossed the valley to come to me. I don't know much about shepherds, but this one was dressed in a fine robe, much like the priest's wear," Joseph explained.

Mary was intrigued. "What did he look like?"

"He looked about my age, with a very fine, almost bony face," Joseph continued. "He had no beard, but that wasn't the strangest thing. It was pouring rain, and my coat was getting soaked. But his robe was not getting wet at all, not even his feet."

"How could that be?" Mary wondered.

"I didn't know, but when he spoke, then I knew," Joseph answered.

"He spoke to you?" Mary asked, fully engaged in his story.

"He did." Joseph's voice grew more intense. "This shepherd, this angel I believe, called me by name. He told me to not be afraid to take you as my wife."

Mary tried to suppress the emotions that welled up inside her as she asked, "He knew who I was?"

"He did," Joseph assured her. "He knew everything. He told me that the child you are carrying was from the Most High and I was to call his name Yeshua."

"Yeshua?" Mary could not hold back the tears any longer.

"Yeshua," Joseph said thoughtfully. "Because he will save his people from their sins, whatever that means."

Joseph noticed that Mary was getting upset and motioned for her to sit down on a low stone wall to rest.

"And then the strangest thing happened," Joseph continued as he sat beside her. "This shepherd angel walked back to his flock and a little lamb escaped, ran right past him and up the hill towards me. I grabbed the wet and shivering lamb to shield it from the rain, and as soon as I did, I was no longer getting wet. My coat was completely dry as I sheltered this little lamb. Then I awoke."

"What did all that mean?" Mary asked through her tears.

"I'm not sure," Joseph said. "But it was like this little lamb I was to care for was like the child, I mean, this son you are having. He is not mine, but he will be mine to care for."

"Oh, Joseph!" Mary cried and her shoulders began to shake with sobs. "There is so much I should have told you!"

"You didn't have to, Mary." Joseph consoled her. "The Most High has told me himself. You are my beloved, and my betrothed, and nothing is going to change that."

Joseph reached over and held her face in his hands. He tried to wipe the tears from her face, but they would not stop flowing.

"I should have told you!" Mary sobbed as she buried her face into his shoulder, months of pondering and worry flowing out of her heart.

Joseph held her for a long while until he decided they would have to head back to make it home by sunset. On the walk home, she told him about the angel visiting her, all the prophecies exchanged between her and Elisabeth, the miracles surrounding the birth of John and all the worries that had plagued her heart.

They reached her door just as the sun was going down.

"When did you make that baby basket you sent for Elisabeth?" Mary had almost forgotten to ask him about that.

"I started it the morning after my dream," Joseph told her as a smile spread across his face. "I figured if I was to be a father, then a carpenter like me should learn to make his child a place to sleep."

"Was that your way of sending a message to me, as well as a gift for Elisabeth?" Mary questioned him.

"Did you think it was a message?" Joseph teased her.

"I was hoping it was a good sign," Mary admitted.

"Then it was," Joseph confirmed. And with that he walked away, laughing as he went.

Mary turned to enter the house and reached for the latch. For months she had dreaded returning home knowing the turmoil that would erupt in her heart every time she turned the latch. She smiled, knowing that she had nothing to fear. Joseph had fixed the latch, just as he had fixed her heart as well.

Chapter Seventeen
The Decree to Bethlehem

The months passed quickly for Mary after returning to Nazareth. She kept herself busy preparing all the items she would need as a bride and secretly sewing the blankets and clothing she would need for her son. Caleb had arranged for her to continue being the seamstress for the synagogue and so she had a constant supply of hems and embroidery to do. No one, apparently, had the time to do the quality work that Mary could, and they had celebrated her return from Judea with more work than she cared to do.

As her middle swelled, she kept changing garments and so far no one other than Caleb and Joseph knew she was with child. She was afraid her walk, especially when carrying a water pot on her head or a heavy basket, would give her condition away. She wondered how long she could keep it a secret, especially when it came time for her to deliver and she would need to arrange for the assistance of a midwife. Then everyone would know and she would bring shame upon herself and Joseph.

There was no way to avoid a public scandal. Even if Joseph had consummated the betrothal with a wedding ceremony as soon as she returned to Nazareth, everyone would soon figure out when the baby was born that she must have been with child before the marriage. The news of their betrothal was no secret. Everyone expected them to complete the marriage as soon as Joseph was ready to take her into his home, but no one expected a child, especially one that came from outside the marriage union.

For his part, Joseph calmed all of Mary's fears about his intentions for her. They talked often of Mary's experiences and how they had been confirmed by his dream. He was ready to take her as his wife, and ready to raise the son they were to call Yeshua. The only part of Joseph's plan he had difficulty giving up on was his dream to build the home on the northern slope of Nazareth.

Before his dream, Joseph considered divorcing Mary quietly before their marriage union so as not to bring shame upon her. After his dream, he was determined to take Mary as his wife, but struggled as he realized that if they married and stayed in Nazareth, when Mary's son was born, everyone would know that she had been with child before their coming together. How could he answer the questions he would surely be asked. Was it his child? He would have to say no. Then whose? Who would believe it was a child of the Most High, as they were told? There was no answer that would not bring shame upon Mary, the very thing Joseph was trying to avoid in the first place.

So Joseph decided with much difficulty that he could not continue his plans to build a house in Nazareth. He did not want to put all his earnings and labour into a home they may never be able to live in. They might have to move to raise their family elsewhere to avoid questions that had no easy answers.

It was a month from the time Joseph decided what he must do before he finally forced himself to visit the farmer and sell back the aging olive grove. While it had been difficult to feel his dream of building a home was dying when he didn't think Mary was returning, it was much more difficult to intentionally put an end to it himself. But he did it, as hard as it was. He did it for Mary. He would do anything for her, realizing that he loved her more than he loved his own plans.

It took Joseph a week to tell Mary what he had done. He wanted to have an alternative plan before talking to her. Mary's condition made her vulnerable enough, and as her husband he was obligated to offer her a secure place to live. Joseph had talked to Caleb and arranged to live in their house if no suitable alternative could be found by the time their union was sealed. Caleb had realized this would be highly unusual but knew that at least his sister would have a place to live, even if it meant he would have to delay his plan to sell the house and move to Jerusalem.

Once Mary was advised of the change in plans, the next step was to plan the wedding event. It was custom for the groom to spend months—even a year—preparing his home for his bride. Whether it was a room at his father's house or a new location, he was responsible for outfitting it with all the furnishings that the new couple would need to commence their life together.

But Joseph's situation was not customary. He would move into the bride's home which was already furnished and functioning. There was almost nothing for him to prepare, so there was no reason to delay the wedding. But still he hesitated.

There had been enough drama in this betrothal already. Rushing into the wedding ceremony might complicate things further. The miracle of Mary's pregnancy was a caution to Joseph. How could he lay with Mary knowing all that had happened to her? And what if his being with her somehow ruined all that was going to happen?

So he committed to not touch her until she had given birth. The marriage ceremony might as well wait. That would give them time to figure out what having a son of the Most High really meant. How he wished the angels had just laid out a list of instructions for them: this is when you marry; here is where you are to live; this is what you tell people when they ask about the boy. Not sure what to do, and not wanting to make wrong choices, they paused their plans for the wedding ceremony.

Late into her eighth month, rumours started to circulate around the village well. Caravans from the west brought news of a new tax that their Roman rulers were going to extract. As long as everyone lived peaceably the Romans left the Galileans to live their lives and practice their religion as they saw fit. The local centurion in charge of the soldiers in the area was a reasonable man who wanted no trouble in his territory. To this end, he caused little trouble himself and the locals gave him due respect.

But the tax collectors were a different story. The officials from Rome taxed the population, supposedly in exchange for their protection and maintaining the main trade routes. Everyone knew it was just a tax on a conquered population that could do little to resist. To expedite the process, the Romans employed locals who spoke the language to collect the taxes for them. Treated as traitors to their own people, these tax collectors were unscrupulous in their methods, routinely charging more than required to fill their own purses.

The talk of a new tax was met with hostility. Soon enough, the rumours were confirmed with edicts from Rome and they learned this was going to be more than just a new tax.

Quirinus, a newly installed governor of the region, had decided that a census should be taken of the Jewish people, to determine the population and expedite the levels of taxation. Though proposed years earlier, it had thankfully never been implemented. But Rome had now given approval and the census would be documented by tribal ancestry.

Though overruled by Rome, the Jewish nation was a kingdom of tribal people. Everyone took great pride in their ancestry. Ever since the time of Joshua the land had been divided amongst the twelve sons of Jacob. They were free to live wherever they wanted in the country but always knew what tribe they belonged to and where their ancestral home was. When a woman was married, she joined the tribe of her husband as did their children. Quirinus thought that a census based on this tribal history would be the most efficient for a relatively small and often nomadic population.

And so began the great exodus of people throughout the country as men travelled to register their name in the towns of their ancestors. They were given six months to comply and receive their certificate of registration. This gave men time to get their crops in, or make arrangements for their families and businesses. Often families would travel with the men, taking advantage of the opportunity to visit relatives and the land of their ancestors.

Almost half of the men of Nazareth were not from the tribe of Manasseh, within whose boundaries Nazareth was situated. Many of them left immediately upon the issued edict, wanting to get it over with and back to their families. Just as many men and families poured into Nazareth which was big enough to have a registry.

The constant movement of people, the officials doing the census work, and the extra Roman soldiers sent to keep order meant the village well and market were active almost any time of day or night.

This allowed Mary to move about in public without much notice, despite her advancing pregnancy.

This also meant Caleb would have to travel to Jerusalem—not a problem for him as he was in the city every couple of months trading anyway. But he wasn't sure if he wanted to leave Mary alone in her condition. Because Joseph had not yet married her, he would be unable to be of any assistance to her when it was her time to give birth. Caleb did not want to leave Mary alone to face possible scorn from the women.

Joseph was from the tribe of Judah, and so he would have to travel to Bethlehem, in the hill country of Judea. He too, was ambivalent about when to go. He could leave immediately and be back within a Sabbath, well before Mary was expecting to give birth. Or he could wait until after the birth and they were officially married.

Although the groom would not normally visit the home of his bride during the months of preparation for the wedding, Caleb convinced Joseph that there was nothing normal about this betrothal anyways, and they could break with tradition. The village was so consumed with the activities of visitors that no one would notice Joseph coming for a visit.

They arranged to meet over an evening meal and discuss how the situation could be handled to everyone's benefit. After much discussion weighing the advantages of various scenarios, the men could still not decide the best thing to do. Mary had listened quietly, letting the men talk it out, but she surprised both of them when she summoned the courage to join the conversation.

"I know you are both trying to protect me, and I appreciate that," she began. "But I think I know what I want to do."

"And what would that be, dear sister?" Caleb asked.

"I think I should go with Joseph," Mary ventured hesitantly.

"What?" Caleb protested. "Why would you want to travel with a new baby?"

"Not with a baby," Mary corrected him. "I'd go with him now, before the baby comes."

It was Joseph's turn to protest. "Mary, I can't possibly let you travel four or five days in your condition! What if something were to happen?"

"And how can you leave with a man who you have not officially married?" Caleb added. "Will there be no end to the shame of the house of Caleb?"

"There will be no shame," Mary explained. "The town is so full of visitors that no one would notice I was gone. And if they did, you could tell them I left with Joseph to be married in the house of his fathers."

"That would solve the dilemma of when to be married," Joseph added, surprising himself by agreeing with Mary.

"And how will you travel?" Caleb demanded.

Mary was quick to answer. "The roads are full of travellers, Caleb. Almost all of them strangers to us. We would just be part of the group. As far as anyone would know, they would think we were already married."

"But you are not," Caleb reminded her.

Joseph rose to Mary's defence. "It is true what Mary says, Caleb. She will travel safely if everyone assumes we are married. And we are betrothed. The leaders of the synagogue tell us that it is as binding as marriage."

Caleb did not challenge him so Joseph continued. "I have no

intention of being with Mary. Not until she has given birth and we have had the wedding ceremony."

"Don't you see, Caleb?" Mary pleaded with him. "By the time Joseph has registered in Bethlehem, it will be close to my time. Elisabeth's house is only a few hours from there, and we can stay with her until I deliver my son. Before I left, Zechariah himself told me that I was welcome in his home any time."

The scattered thoughts of her heart over the past months were now falling into place like pieces of a puzzle. Why her and Elizabeth should both be with child only months apart. Why staying with Elizabeth for months now made more sense than ever. Why Joseph would have to travel to the hill country of Judea just now. How she would be able to give birth to this child without shaming Caleb or herself. She blurted it all out as the men listened, too amazed at her plan to interrupt.

"If I have my son at Elizabeth's, she can be my midwife as well as any of the other women I have met there," Mary explained breathlessly. "Elizabeth knows I am with child, and that it is not Joseph's, so there is no shame there. Zechariah is a priest and can do the circumcision. We could stay there until it is time for me to go to Jerusalem to present the offerings. Then we could have the wedding ceremony and return to Nazareth. By that time we are married and have a son. There will no shame for any of us." Mary finished abruptly, aware that as a bride she should not be planning her own wedding.

No one said anything for long minutes until Caleb finally spoke. "And what if you have difficulty in travelling?" Caleb's tone was no longer critical, but concerned. "What if something happens on the road?"

Joseph, who had been listening with amazement, suddenly came up with a plan of his own. "I have the money from the sale of the land," Joseph offered. "It's enough for us to travel with, and maybe enough to buy a donkey for Mary to ride on, if she is able, or to carry our provisions so it is easier for us to walk. With a donkey, we could carry the extra supplies Mary will need for the child. We could even sell the donkey once in Judea when we no longer needed it to pay for a wedding ceremony."

Caleb laughed, as much to relieve tension as in delight. "I am pleased to see that you have taken some lessons from me in trading! I may make a merchant out of you yet!"

Caleb's laughter relaxed them all, and they stopped examining the options, talking late into the night as they discussed what each of them would do to make Mary's plan a reality. Mary would begin to prepare the food and provisions they would need to travel. Caleb would find a donkey for Joseph to purchase. He would send word on the next caravan to Jedidiah in Jerusalem for him to tell Elisabeth that Mary was returning. Joseph would finish up the jobs he was working on and not take on any new work, since he would be gone for weeks, maybe longer. Because of the census, no one would think this out of the ordinary.

Once Joseph and Mary left, Caleb would wait a couple months before travelling to Jerusalem to register for the census. That way he would only be a few hours journey away from Mary to celebrate the birth of her son, maybe even their marriage if all went as planned. Satisfied that they had it all worked out, Joseph bid farewell to Mary. He would not see her again until they left Nazareth together as betrothed, hoping to return later as husband and wife and father and mother to a little gift from Jehovah.

Chapter Eighteen
The Road to Bethlehem

It only took Joseph a week to wrap up his building projects. The ones he couldn't finish, Obadiah gave to other carpenters who were happy for the work. So many men were either coming or going to Nazareth that steady work was hard to find. It was as if the census had put everyone's lives on hold for a time. Building homes and furniture was not top priority.

He had started building a wooden basket for Mary, just as he had for Elizabeth. He had learned a lot from his first attempt and was going at the project for his own child in painstaking detail. But he would not be able to finish it now, and it would probably be a burden to bring with them anyways. Besides, he reasoned, if Mary was going to give birth at Elisabeth's then she would have the chance to use hers, at least for a short time.

As Joseph tidied his shop, he debated whether to take any of his small hand tools with him. Perhaps Zechariah would need fixing up at the house and he could help him with that as thanks for all he had done for Mary. He decided to take a mallet, a chisel, and a small draw knife. The knife could be used for meals as well as work, so he packed them into his sack and hoped Mary would not mind.

Caleb took Jospeh's money and negotiated to purchase a donkey for their journey. He used what was left over to buy a decent harness lead and a satchel that would sit like a saddle, hanging over each side of the donkey, holding many of their provisions. Mary could also ride the donkey with the satchel still attached.

Mary used her final week in Nazareth to finish up all the sewing for the synagogue leaders. When she delivered the baskets of sewing she wondered if anyone noticed she waddled a little when she walked. She made sure to keep her shoulders straight and tried not to sway when she stepped. This only made her back hurt more, so she was glad she would not have to make such efforts on the journey to Judea. She would be able to walk in whatever manner she was comfortable without being self-conscious about it.

She assembled all the clothing, blankets, and headscarves she would need for the journey. As she did, she thought of how she had prepared for this same journey only eight months before. So much had happened since then. Last time she left in confusion about what was happening to her, in fear about her relationship with Joseph. This time, though still confused about what having this son was going to mean, she was no longer fearful. Joseph was still her beloved and they were going to face this future together, whatever it may bring.

They prepared to leave the day after the Sabbath. They were sure to make it to Bethlehem to register and on to Elisabeth's before the next Sabbath. That way they would not have to celebrate a Sabbath while travelling, which would mean an extra day on the road with no progress. Mary prepared as much bread and meal as they would need for the Sabbath day and their journey. She went to the market for the last time and bought some fruit and dried fish, wondering if this is what her ancestors must have gone through while wandering in the desert—always preparing food for a journey and never knowing if it would be enough to last. No wonder Jehovah sent them manna to eat.

Mary had not seen Joseph since the night they planned their journey. She hoped he would be wise enough to bring a change of clothes, maybe even an extra pair of sandals. She had watched Caleb leave for his journeys with no more than the cloak on his back and a sleeping mat, and wondered why men left so ill prepared. She asked Caleb to check on him and he told her that she worried too much. But Joseph had travelled very little, as far as Mary knew, and it concerned her that he would not be prepared with all the things they may need.

By the evening the Sabbath began, Mary had everything ready. She stayed at home all Sabbath day, trying to rest as much as possible. When Caleb returned from the synagogue, they did not talk much. Just being together as brother and sister was enough. By the time Caleb saw her again, she would likely be a married woman and a mother. As much as Caleb approved of her husband and their plan to have the child in Judea, he was sad that the relationship he had with his sister would change forever. She would not be there for him to tease, and he would not hear her laughter. Nothing would ever be the same again, and he knew that he would miss her warm personality and mothering care.

It was already hot when Mary and Caleb met up with Joseph at the village well the next morning. The crowd of travellers had gathered to go as a group down to Jerusalem. Most were families who were returning home after registering in Nazareth. There was only one family from Nazareth travelling to be registered in Judea. The rest were tradesmen or merchants with their donkeys packed with wares. Two Roman soldiers were also going with the group as rumours of bandits on the roads were numerous. They would not travel with the group, as that would be improper, but would travel a quarter mile ahead of the group as guards.

They bid farewell to Caleb, and he promised to meet them at Elisabeth's in a month or so. They were to send word as best they could if the plans changed.

Caleb and Joseph locked forearms, saying nothing, as men often did when saying farewell. Caleb hugged Mary tightly, feeling the pressure of her hidden midsection. He gazed upon her tenderly and then looked away as his eyes filled with tears.

"Now you are the one who is crying," Mary teased him as her eyes flooded as well.

Caleb smiled weakly amidst the braying of donkeys and the sounds of several dialects as the group started off. Joseph tugged on the lead of the donkey and joined the group. Caleb released Mary from his arms and walked with them to the edge of town. He waited there until the group was just a cloud of dust in the distance, praying that Mary would be safe on the road and in her future.

Mary decided to walk as much as she was able in the morning, and then ride the donkey if she grew tired. They did not know the other family from Nazareth by name, so Mary was relieved that she did not have to monitor how she walked. She fell into a rhythm of swaying slightly from side to side which helped her back not to hurt. At a turn in the road or the crest of hill, she would often think how she had already travelled this route twice in the past nine months, and all the memories of how she felt at those times would flood back to her.

Lost in thought, she didn't talk much to Joseph that first day. He seemed content to lead the donkey, periodically asking her how she was doing. When the sun was high, they rested for a bit as the men watered their animals and everyone broke bread to eat. When they started off again, Joseph convinced Mary to ride the donkey, at least for a short while to see if it was comfortable for her. She obliged, and as he clumsily lifted her onto the beast's back, she noticed how effortlessly his strong arms and broad shoulders handled her. He almost seemed embarrassed to hold her in his arms, since he had not held her for months. Mary blushed as well, and smiled back at him, hoping that no one in the group noticed the awkwardness between them.

Mary rode the donkey for the rest of the afternoon. The gait was uneven, and often Joseph would have to tug on the beast to keep it moving. But it was giving her legs a rest, even if her back hurt with the bouncing up and down as much as it would if she were walking. They travelled towards the back of the group of about thirty people. Some had joined them on the way, and there was talk of others leaving once they reached the road along the Jordan Valley to cross over the river to the other side.

Once they reached the main route along the Jordan, the plan was to stay at the khan about an hour's journey south.

As they travelled the last hour of the day, Mary began to talk about her experiences on earlier trips this way and what they could expect. Joseph replied hesitantly at first, but eased into the conversation as they went. Soon they were talking comfortably with each other, occasionally teasing and laughing as they used to do, with the antics of the donkey inspiring much of the conversation.

This was all new territory for them. They were alone for the first time in each other's company and as far as anyone knew, were husband and wife. Legally they were, except for the ceremony, but in practice they were not.

Mary could tell by the landscape that they were near the khan and would soon be stopping for the night, so she initiated the conversation about the sleeping arrangements. Joseph slowed the pace of the donkey so they fell back from the group a bit to talk.

As they had discussed, everyone travelling with them assumed they were married. Their travelling companions had noticed that Mary was with child, as she had made no attempt to hide the fact. No one really asked any questions out of the ordinary, and most just congratulated the young couple. Now they must spend the night together, and Joseph insisted that he would not lay with her. Mary agreed without hesitation. But they needed to appear to be in a normal marriage relationship, not wanting to raise any suspicions to the contrary.

They decided to wait until they reached the khan to see if everyone would have their own sleeping quarters. With all the travelling of the population because of the census, it might be overflowing with guests anyways. They arrived just in time to get their own stall for the donkey, and a sleeping loft above. They planned to eat their evening meal with the group around the well, which was normal. Then Joseph would help Mary up the stairs to her sleeping mat. He would return to join the men around the fire to talk into the night, just as Caleb would. Once it was completely dark, he would join Mary in the loft, sleeping with their provisions between them.

This would be completely out of character for Joseph, who would sooner sit in the stall with the donkey and whittle with his knife than join a conversation about politics, farming, and religion. But he did the best he could, and was glad that neither he nor Mary became the topic of conversation. They did ask about his donkey, as they had noticed his lack of skill in handling the beast. He admitted he was a carpenter and not a farmer and had no experience with such a cantankerous animal. They joked about how he needed to treat the beast as he would his wife, and order it about. Such talk made Joseph uncomfortable, and he was glad when it was dark enough for him to escape.

As he crept quietly into the loft, he could hear Mary's steady breathing and was sure that she had fallen asleep. He groped about in the dim light that the far off fire provided, not wanting to light the lamp they had brought in case it disturbed Mary. He could not find his sleeping mat or blanket where he thought he had left them, until he realized Mary had already rolled it out and had his blanket and pillow ready for him.

How kind, he thought as he removed his cloak and lay down. Listening to Mary's breathing, he thought of all the plans he had for this woman. How many of them might never come to pass because the Most High had interrupted his plans. Now his concern was how to maintain her honour while they travelled and eventually delivered their son.

He tried to think of anyone else who had been put in this predicament. He thought of the patriarch Isaac and how his wife was brought to him from another country. He thought of his namesake, Joseph, but could find nothing in his life to compare. Then he remembered his ancestor, Boaz. Before she was his wife, Ruth came and lay at Boaz's feet to indicate her wish for him to marry her.

Quietly, Joseph repositioned his mat as best he could so his feet were facing the mat where Mary continued to sleep, stirring occasionally. Satisfied that he was following the precedent of his ancestors, Joseph lay in the dark, and the rhythm of Mary's breathing rocked him into a dreamless sleep.

Chapter Nineteen

On the Jericho Road

The braying of the animals crying to be fed, the pungent smoke of the morning fires, and the shouts of the men as they began their day made it impossible to sleep past dawn in the khan. Joseph rose before Mary and went to the well to get her a fresh jug of water. She was awake by the time he returned. Not sure if he should see her before she refreshed herself, he backed into the sleeping quarters and left the jug without looking at her.

While Joseph attended to the donkey, Mary rose from her mat, smiling at Joseph's shyness. Caleb needn't have feared that Joseph would disrespect her. She couldn't even remember when he came to sleep and he was gone before she was awake. She noticed as she dressed for the day that his mat had been turned sideways. *Strange carpenter,* she thought, *and sweet.*

Joseph had the donkey fed and readied for the day and he went to gather their belongings. He made sure Mary was aware he was coming by telling the donkey he was going up the stairs. Mary heard him and decided to ease the tension.

"We are talking to donkeys now, Joseph?"

"Of course," Joseph replied as he climbed the stairs. "It is what I learned from the others around the fire last night. You must get the

The Love of Mary

beast used to the sound of your voice, not just when you are ordering it about."

Joseph reached the top of the stairs and could not help but stare as Mary finished tucking her hair into her headscarf. She was as beautiful as ever, but in the last months her face had matured into the radiance of womanhood. *She is wonderful to behold, even first thing in the morning,* Joseph thought, then he realized his staring might make her uncomfortable. "Did you sleep well last night?" he ventured, breaking out of his trance.

"Yes, I actually did," Mary replied. "My back is a little sore, but that is to be expected."

"Good," Joseph nodded as he rolled up his mat. "I mean, not good that your back is sore, but good that you slept."

"And did you sleep at all?" Mary asked in an accusing voice.

"Yes, of course, why wouldn't I?" Joseph responded in kind.

"I just noticed that your mat was turned sideways, as if you were uncomfortable and had trouble sleeping," Mary explained.

Joseph finished tying up his mat and hesitated, not sure whether to tell Mary about his reasons. She would think him foolish, but she might as well know why, since he was likely to do the same thing every time they slept.

"I was thinking about how we should sleep together, without being together," Joseph confessed. "I thought of my ancestors Boaz and Ruth, and how before they were married, she slept at his feet."

"That is so sweet, Joseph." Mary smiled at this rough but sensitive man. "And as long as you wash your feet before lying down on your mat, I have no problem with that."

Joseph paused, then realized she was teasing him and he laughed out loud. Together they chuckled as they bundled up their belongings and went down the stairs.

After some bread and meal, they packed up the donkey and joined the group that had assembled for departure. As Joseph boosted Mary onto the donkey and her feet brushed against his arm, he reciprocated the earlier teasing. "Maybe you should wash your feet as well," he said, as he helped her settle onto the beast.

She laughed at his suggestion as Joseph tugged at the donkey's lead to start the day's journey.

The main road following the Jordan River valley was as dusty as ever, and the caravan left a cloud behind them that hung in the air in every valley. *Much like the cloud that led the Israelites through the desert,* Joseph thought. He had not travelled as much as Mary and the sights, sounds, and smells of the journey both delighted and repulsed him. Sharing many of these thoughts with Mary as they travelled relaxed them both after the awkwardness of their first night together.

There was no khan to stay in for the second night on their journey. They took shelter against a high ledge of rocks that offered some protection for the animals. Each of the group found their own place along the rocky wall to lay down their supplies and spread out their sleeping mats. The men piled some rocks to make a fire pit and set it to burning. Around this the group gathered and ate their evening meal, sharing stories of their lives.

Mary had become increasingly sore as the day went on. She even walked the last couple hours of the day as the she grew tired of bouncing on the donkey's back. Now squatting by the fire with the women, it was obvious she was uncomfortable. She excused herself from the group and went to lay on her mat before darkness fell.

Joseph noticed her leave the group and went to help. "Are you all right, Mary?" he asked as he supported her back to help her lay down.

"Yes, just a little sore," Mary confessed. "I know riding the donkey keeps me off my feet, but I'm not sure if it is helping my back much."

"Is there anything I can do?" Joseph asked tentatively.

"Maybe if we pile some of the baskets and sacks beside my mat so I can rest my back against them, that would help," Mary proposed.

Joseph did as she suggested and then knelt beside her.

"That is better," Mary said, as she relaxed against the makeshift support. "Thank you."

"It's nothing," Joseph replied. He lay down opposite her and leaned on his elbow to watch over her. He reached over and stroked her forehead with his hand and was pleased to see her relax.

Mary closed her eyes as she felt his rough hands rub her forehead. How long would it be, she wondered, before she was able to reciprocate the tender care that he was giving her? She thought of all that had happened and was yet to come, and drifted off to sleep with Joseph's hand caressing her face.

They awoke to the shouts of the men preparing their beasts for the day's journey. Joseph lifted himself up on one elbow and looked down at his feet where Mary was just awakening herself. Still on her side, resting against their sacks, her dark hair tumbled in a veil over her face. *She is beautiful without even trying,* Joseph thought, and he imagined the morning he would be able to wake up beside her.

As Mary brushed the hair away from her face, Joseph noticed her eyes were open. Embarrassed by his stare, he hastily got up. Without saying a word, he left his mat to join the other men.

Mary tried calling after him, but realized it was awkward for him to wake up with her. *He's so shy,* she thought as she got up on her knees and rubbed her side.

By the time Joseph returned with the donkey, Mary had washed and dressed and was ready to go. They had a few minutes before the group was leaving so they shared some bread and fruit.

"Did you sleep well last night?" Joseph asked.

"I must have. I don't think I moved all night," Mary told him. "And how did you sleep, Boaz?"

Joseph looked at her twinkling eyes and he almost spit out his mouthful of food as he stifled a laugh. Mary had this way of using her sense of humour to ease the tension between them as they learned to live together.

"Much better than last night," Joseph admitted, "because I washed my feet before lying down."

Laughing together at their silly banter, they packed up their belongings and joined the caravan now leaving. Mary decided to walk as long as she could to give her legs and back a stretch. As they walked they talked about all that had happened to them both, and what would happen at Elisabeth's when the baby was born. Mary would have to wait a month for her purification, so travelling was out of the question. Then they would have to offer the sacrifice to consecrate their firstborn at the temple. They might as well stay with Elisabeth until then, and stop at Jerusalem on their way back home to Nazareth.

They talked about whether they would return to Nazareth at all. If Caleb were to sell the house to ply his merchant trade elsewhere, there would be little reason for Mary to return. Joseph was happy to live there, but as a carpenter, could work almost anywhere.

They talked of when the marriage ceremony should take place, and where? Not in Nazareth, possibly at Elisabeth's? Or maybe in Jerusalem at Jedidiah's, after the sacrifice of purification? The talk of Jedidiah presented another problem.

If they spent their night in Jerusalem at Jedidiah's, there would be no way to conceal Mary's pregnancy. How would they explain that? Jedidiah had teased Mary about her carpenter from Nazareth. How could they risk both their reputations with questions they were unable to answer? But if Jedidiah found out there were in Jerusalem and did not stay with him, he could be offended.

Their conversation produced more questions than answers, and they were both relieved when the group stopped for a rest. They couldn't talk with the others close by and it gave them both time to process their conversation.

The group decided they would not push on all the way to Jerusalem as it would be too much for the women and children, and it would mean travelling late into the night. They would stop for the night at the khan at Jericho and have a short journey the third day into Jerusalem. Some of the group were heading east across the Jordan River from Jericho anyways, so a stop there made sense for them.

As they started the walk again, Mary rode the donkey. This meant there was little talking between them as the sun rose high in the early afternoon. This suited Joseph just fine. He felt he had talked too much already for that day. Mary was glad for the time to be lost in her thoughts, much of it spent comparing her mood now with how it was when she took this journey by herself eight months ago.

The khan at Jericho was the best in the land. Herod the Great had built a winter palace here, and so the town catered to wealthy and politically important people. The khan even had private rooms where you could pay for meals and lodging. Even the common area was a welcome relief with a good well and protective sleeping bunks. The rocky landscapes were famous for tales of robbers and wild animals, so the men made sure the livestock was secure in their pens and then built an exceptionally large fire that would burn throughout the night.

Mary and Joseph ate their evening meal of dried fish and fruit. Mary shared with Joseph for the first time all her fears when she took this journey alone; how she didn't know what she would find at Elisabeth's and how he would react. Joseph listened in silence, amazed at how she had struggled through all this mental anguish.

Finally they got around to talking about the plans for the next day.

"I just can't stay at Jedidiah's," Mary was the first to admit. "I know he will find out eventually, but the later the better, I think."

"That's not a problem for me," Joseph confirmed. "I've never met the man so I would like it be as positive as possible. Questions about why you are so heavy with child are not ones I want to answer."

"And what will be our answer, Joseph?" Mary pleaded. "What are we going to tell people?"

Joseph shrugged. "I'm not sure. I could tell them what the angel told me—that this boy would save his people from their sins—but I don't even know what that means."

"The angel told me that he would sit on the throne of our father David, forever," Mary added. "I have no idea what that means, either."

"Those two messages don't even go together," admitted Joseph. "It would be better if we didn't say anything."

"Perhaps Zechariah could help us with this," Mary proposed.

"He is a priest and must know about such things."

"You're right," Joseph agreed. "We can wait until we are at Zechariah's. Not much will happen before then. If we stay at the khans beside the temple, then we will be lost in the crowd, and won't have to explain anything."

"And from Jerusalem, it is only a few hours walk to Bethlehem, even in my condition," Mary offered. "If we leave right after you register, by nightfall we will be at Elizabeth's."

"You have it all planned out, don't you?" teased Joseph. "Now how did you plan to sleep tonight?"

"The same way I did last night," Mary said.

Taking the suggestion, Joseph arranged everything as it was the night before. He brought a fresh bowl of water from the well and some hot rocks from the fire to put at Mary's feet. Once sure she was comfortable, he sat beside her and pulled out his knife. While he whittled away on a piece of wood, he hummed parts of songs he remembered, just as he would have while at work.

"What are you making?" Mary asked before she drifted off to sleep.

"Nothing," Joseph admitted. "It just relaxes me. All this walking and talking make me anxious to do something with my hands."

Mary reached out for his hand, and Joseph put down the knife so as not to hurt her. She put his hand on her face, encouraging him to stroke her forehead as he had the night before. Relaxing his position, he lay down beside her and rubbed her forehead, sometimes twisting her hair around his fingers as she slept. The khan grew quiet as the travellers rested, and with his hand still upon Mary's face, without even intending to, Joseph fell asleep.

Chapter Twenty

Jerusalem

Joseph awoke at the first break of dawn, even before the animals began stirring. He realized he had been sleeping opposite Mary the whole night, not even lying on his mat. Quietly he got up and carefully arranged his mat perpendicular to Mary, who slept soundly, although she stirred occasionally. Realizing he would not be getting back to sleep, he decided to stoke the fire and prepare a hot meal to start the day.

By the time Mary woke to the rising sun reflecting off the sheltering rocks, Joseph had a fresh bowl of warm water for her and had heated up some bread cakes. After eating, Joseph left to prepare the donkey while Mary got ready for the day.

Two families said their farewells as they headed out to cross the Jordan River to their homes in Moab territory. The rest were anxious to start the climb up to Jerusalem, which was several hundred feet higher than where they had camped in the Jordan River valley. The company would make Jerusalem by the ninth hour of the day, which was almost a necessity if they were to find lodging for the night in the bustling city.

Mary could not decide which was hurting her more: her feet or her back. She remembered how just nine months ago she had

The Love of Mary

actually carried a child on this last leg of the journey to Jerusalem. *Surely the child I now carry could not weigh more than the child I carried in my makeshift sling,* she thought, but how much more difficulty she was having!

Joseph realized Mary was struggling, so he rearranged the sacks on the donkey to make a slightly better ride. She had intended to walk for the first hour, but Joseph had gone through so much trouble she decided to ride. They talked very little as he led the donkey up the rocky hills, both lost in their thoughts.

Just after midday, they caught the first view of the bleached rooftops of the city. Wisps of smoke rose above the roofs, hanging in the air like low clouds. The landscape rolled up to meet the city walls on every side as if they were the foundation. In the distance they saw the peaks and parapets of the temple, and beyond that the pinnacles of Herod's temple. It truly was a city set on a hill.

As they entered the city through the gate, Mary climbed off the donkey and walked beside Joseph. The bustle of the narrow city streets never ceased to fascinate her: the sights of the houses and shops that confronted her at every turn; the smells of cooking and produce that she could never escape; the sounds of children playing and merchants hawking their wares, often in dialects she didn't understand; all these both delighted and alarmed her. No wonder Caleb wanted to leave the calm streets of Nazareth and relocate his business to Jerusalem.

Joseph walked in silence beside her, maneuvering the donkey to avoid the other people and carts and beasts that paid no attention to other travellers on the street. He had not travelled much, and had only been to Jerusalem a few times in his whole life. The frantic activity of the streets annoyed him, mostly because it prevented him from paying attention to the architecture of the city. He would admire the stonework of one building, only to be horrified at the poor workmanship of the door and mantle on the one next to it.

They needed to decide where to spend the night in the city. With an early start the next day, they would be able to get to Bethlehem by noon. Joseph could register for the census and they could easily make it to Elisabeth's house by the supper hour.

"Should we stay with your uncle Zedediah, or not?" Joseph finally broke the silence that the hustle of the city had seduced them into.

"And if we did, how would we explain my condition?" Mary replied thoughtfully. "I was just at his house less than six months ago, and if I were to present myself now, what would I say? I thought we already decided this."

"He is sure to find out once the child is born." Joseph reasoned. "Will it be any easier to explain then?"

"Perhaps not," Mary pondered aloud. "But a baby changes everything. I saw that with Elizabeth. Once little John was born, all the questions and confusion didn't matter anymore. The joy of birth is overwhelming for everyone and all the focus is on the child. Everything else seems of little importance."

"So a baby changes everything. And I thought it was the baby that would need all the changing." Joseph laughed as he put his arm around Mary to squeeze her shoulder as she clucked in mock dismay at his humour. "All right then, we will spend the denarii to find a room at a khan." Joseph conceded. "You have been here much more than me. Do you know where one might be?"

"There are always lots near the temple to accommodate all the visitors at feast times," Mary offered. "There are no festivals right now, so I am sure we will find a room."

"If this is how busy the city is without flocks of visitors, how crazy will it be when they come?" Joseph wondered.

"Well, there could be extra travellers for the census, just as we are," Mary answered. "We are not the only ones inconvenienced at this time."

"An inconvenience for sure," Joseph agreed. "But at the same time, convenient for you, to have your baby at Elizabeth's. Actually, convenient for both of us, now that I think of it."

"Really, Joseph?" Mary was surprised to hear him talk like that. "Convenient for you to leave your trade and give up plans to build a house? To leave for months, maybe more?"

"Really, Mary," Joseph answered confidently. "Staying in Nazareth would have caused a lot of awkward situations. I'm just as glad to leave for a while, as long as I have you with me."

It was Mary this time who laughed with delight as she reached out an arm to Joseph, who willingly took it. Leaning on him as she tired of walking, Mary and Joseph continued down the streets of the city towards the temple. To the people they passed, they looked like just another couple almost too young to be married, expecting a child, and hopelessly in love.

The outer courts of the temple were within sight when they started seeing the makeshift signs that people had posted offering everything that someone might need for a visit to the temple. Prayer shawls, scrolls of scripture, turtledoves for sacrifice, and an endless number of bowls, garments, and trinkets. The signs soon gave way to hawkers who were not content to stay in the doorway of their shops or homes but mingled with the crowd on the street, extolling the virtues of their offerings.

Joseph and Mary pushed through the crowds until they reached the collection of khans just south of the temple, situated to appeal to the travellers coming from the south and the seacoast. The first two they stopped at were full, or were expected to be so, and would not give up any spaces. At the third they were able to secure a shelter for the donkey and a sleeping loft, but not for the denarii Joseph was expecting. Two denarii a night was the going rate, and Joseph's feeble attempt at bargaining was to no avail. It only resulted in an extra charge for the donkey since Joseph had run out of food for his beast.

"This is the type of situation where I need Caleb to do the bargaining for me," Joseph said, as they unpacked the donkey and tied him in the stall.

"I'm not sure even Caleb would have much success with these merchants," Mary offered as consolation. "You found me a place to rest, and that is enough. I'm not sure I could walk another step."

"Well, just a few more up to the sleeping loft," Joseph encouraged her, extending a hand to help her up the stone steps. Once Mary had reached the loft, Joseph retrieved their sleeping mats and helped Mary get comfortable.

"I'll find something for us to eat," Joseph offered. "You just lie here and rest."

"We have some bread left over, I'm sure," Mary reminded him.

"It's three days old now, and I'm not even sure the donkey would want it," Joseph teased. "You did a great job making enough food to get us this far. Tomorrow night we will be at Elisabeth's, so we can buy enough for one more day."

"All right," Mary conceded. "If I fall asleep, wake me when you return. I am more tired than hungry, but I should eat before night falls, I am sure."

"I will. See you in a little while," Joseph promised as he walked down the steps.

It was past the twelfth hour when Joseph ventured back into the heart of Jerusalem. The streets in his hometown of Nazareth would be quiet by now, but here the people still thronged about. Some still came and went from the temple courts, which seemed as much as a tourist attraction as a place of worship. Merchant tables were set up at every approach to the temple selling wares and creatures of all kinds.

Joseph avoided these and headed to the shops offering bread, fish, dates, and cakes. He wandered about for quite a time, curious about the varieties of food available in the city and fascinated by all the types of people, their dress and language. Speech was peppered with colloquialisms he wasn't sure he understood.

He didn't notice how late it was getting until long shadows made the tapestry of the city dim. He hurried to purchase the food as the shopkeepers quickly took away their goods as night fell.

Mary was asleep when Joseph returned, and he laid out some bread and dates before he woke her. She grimaced a smile as she propped herself up on her side so she could eat with Joseph.

"With an early start in the morning, could we be at Elisabeth's by tomorrow night?" Joseph asked as he sat opposite Mary.

"It is only a few hours journey as I remember," she replied.

"Even in your condition?" teased Joseph.

"Even in my condition, as you call it," Mary pretended to scold him. "But I don't know how long you will take to register in Bethlehem."

"Hopefully only an hour," Joseph ventured. "If it is too busy, we could always continue on to Elisabeth's, and then I could return to Bethlehem to register the next day."

"You could do that," Mary agreed. "It would only be a few hours back to Bethlehem, even in your condition."

"And what condition would that be?" Joseph challenged her.

"Oh, a nervous, expectant father, who is overattentive and doting to the mother of his child," Mary remarked.

"You say that as if it is a bad way to be," Joseph pretended to be offended.

"And I wouldn't want it any other way," Mary smiled as she broke a date and offered half to Joseph.

"As strange as our situation is, I can't think of having it any other way," Joseph agreed.

"Really, Joseph?"

"Really, Mary."

They finished their late evening snack, and Mary settled back down on her mat. Joseph lovingly covered her with his cloak to help take off the chill of the night air before he arranged his own mat so his feet would be at her side.

Laying awake until he was sure Mary was asleep, Joseph planned out the next few days. Tomorrow he would register, and then they would go to stay with Elisabeth and Zechariah. In a few days or so the boy would be born and Zechariah could do the circumcision. They would have to travel back to Jerusalem for the ritual of Mary's purification and then they could continue on home to Nazareth. Then, and only then, would Joseph finally be able to take Mary as his wife.

This final thought pleased him the most and with the vision of finally having his betrothed as his wife racing through his mind, he fell asleep.

Chapter Twenty-One
Bethlehem

It was Mary who woke first this time, but it wasn't the noise of the city, the braying of the animals, or the smoke of the first wood fires of the day. She woke before dawn feeling nauseous, and first thought it must have been the dates. But the cramping she felt was not from indigestion, and she quickly remembered how Elisabeth had felt before John was born and knew that her time was coming soon.

She got up in the dark without waking Joseph and picked her way down the stairs to go refresh herself. She cramped once again on her way back up the stairs, and had to pause to regain her composure. Thankfully she got back to her mat without waking Joseph, and lay there as the darkness slowly gave way to the grey of dawn, wondering about all that was about to happen and how she and Joseph were going to manage.

She lay, pondering until she noticed Joseph stirring. She pretended to be sleeping, noticing how carefully he got up from his mat so as not to disturb her. He went silently down the stairs and she could hear him attending to the donkey and arranging things for the day. She got up and began to put away their blankets and sleeping mats by the time Joseph returned to their quarters.

"Did you sleep well, Mary?" Joseph asked.

"Well, but not much," Mary answered truthfully.

"Why is that?" Joseph asked, and then quickly realized the answer and said in a low voice "Oh, I see."

"It's only one more day," Mary reassured him. "I'll make it."

"That is good to hear," Joseph tried to sound confident. "We're not really prepared to have the baby here."

"Then let's be on our way," Mary encouraged him. "I'm not hungry just now. I will have something once we are on the road."

Joseph gathered up their sleeping gear and headed down the stairs. Halfway down, he stopped to make sure Mary followed close behind so if she missed a step she could lean on him. They had made it this far without an incident and Joseph was determined to keep it that way until they were safely at Elisabeth's.

Not taking the time to eat in the morning gave them an early start ahead of other travellers so they were mostly alone on the road out of Jerusalem. It was only a few hours of walking to Bethlehem, but Mary tired quickly and Joseph tried to convince her to ride the donkey. She knew the jostling about would only hasten what she felt was already happening within her, so she persuaded him that walking was more comfortable.

The heights of Jerusalem soon gave way to the rolling country hills of Judea. It was impossible for Mary not to remember all that was going through her heart and mind when she made this journey alone only six months ago. The fear and confusion she felt as she had journeyed to Elisabeth's was only compounded on the way back to Nazareth by the uncertainty of Joseph's reaction when she returned home.

"How are you doing, Mary?" Joseph broke into her thoughts.

"I'm all right, just not walking as quickly as I could a few days ago," Mary admitted.

"You walk just as slowly as you need to," Joseph assured her. "We can stop as often as you want for a rest."

"Maybe now would be good," Mary suggested as she sat on an outcropping of rock that jutted into the road. Joseph secured the donkey to a bramble and brought her a flask of water. While she drank, he busied himself with the donkey and their belongings, unsure of what to do to help her.

Mary was aware of Joseph's awkwardness in this situation which was new to both of them. She still felt occasional cramping and did her best to not let Joseph notice her discomfort. When she saw that Joseph had stopped fidgeting with their load and was growing impatient, she suggested that she was ready to continue.

As they walked along, Mary started up a conversation to distract her from her discomfort and to ease any tension that Joseph might feel from their slowing pace. She talked of all the times she had travelled to visit Elisabeth with Caleb and her parents. As she was talking about the trips they had made with Zechariah to Bethlehem to arrange for temple sheep, a group of shepherd boys came over the hill herding a small flock onto the road towards them.

Joseph interrupted her. "Mary, do you remember the dream I told you about?"

"Yes, I remember," Mary assured him.

"That's the lamb. That's the one right there!" Joseph pointed as he spoke.

As the shepherds drew closer to them, Mary could see a few lambs with their ewes but they all looked the same to her. She didn't dare admit that to Joseph, who handed her the donkey's tether so he could go meet the shepherds.

Mary watched with amazement and amusement as Joseph spoke with the shepherds and assured them he did not want to rob nor buy a lamb. He only wanted to hold one, and after some discussion they allowed him to do so. He picked up the little lamb and held its bleating face to his own. Mary had never seen any man, not even Zechariah, act in such a manner. Apparently, neither had the shepherd boys who giggled amongst themselves as this rough looking grown man cuddled the lamb like it was a baby.

Joseph was oblivious to their reaction and after a couple minutes released the lamb to its mother. Mary had heard his story, but not until now did she realize how much his dream had influenced his reaction to her pregnancy. He really believed God had spoken to him in the dream, just as much as she believed God had spoken to her with the visit from the angel.

Joseph reached out to take the tether from her without saying a word. Mary did not know what to say. She did not want to ruin this encounter which had clearly touched him deeply. She reached out to touch his face and with her fingers gently wiped what could have been a tear. She coaxed his face down to hers, pressing her cheek against his beard. As the shepherd boys passed them on the road, they giggled again at the sight of this young couple embracing in the middle of the road.

Their pace quickened as they resumed their walk, as if the bond between them that was strengthened by the encounter with the lamb had given them new energy. As they reached the crest of the last hill before the path to Bethlehem veered east off the main road, they stopped to rest. The village was in clear view below them, its cream-coloured roofs gleaming in the sun. Wisps of smoke rose above the village and hugged the hills as if shrouded in fog. Flocks of sheep dotted the landscape like low lying clouds. Far to the east they could see the palace that Herod had build in the wilderness. Herodium was his desert retreat and overlooked the hill country like a sentry on watch.

It was almost the sixth hour and the road was busy now with travellers in both directions. Joseph and Mary shared some dried fruit and then rose to walk the last half hour to Bethlehem. If registering went quickly, they might even make it to Elizabeth's by the evening meal.

They were surprised at the many travellers who were also taking the fork in the road that led to Bethlehem. There couldn't be more than a few hundred people who lived in Bethlehem, yet there seemed to be as many on the road that day. Certainly there would be a lot of descendants who would trace their ancestry to the City of David. *Surely they wouldn't all converge on the village at the same time,* Joseph hoped as they descended the last hill to the village. For her part, Mary was trying to not let Joseph notice she was waddling as much as walking now. Cramps continued to grip her as she did all she could to not draw attention to that fact.

Bethlehem was an old town, and many of the buildings were a testament to its history. Some upper portions of walls were crumbling, and many of the wooden features of doors, windows, and roof beams were deteriorating. They made their way to the village well where they were sure to get information about registering. Sure enough, the Romans had set up a tent nearby where a long line was forming and moving very slowly. Joseph found a shady spot to tie up the donkey where Mary could stay off her feet, and he went to join the line.

Mary shifted uncomfortably as she watched Joseph move slowly up the line of registrants. They had made it this far and once Joseph finished, they only had few hours of walking to do. How glad she would be to arrive at Elisabeth's and finally be able to relax. The incident with the lamb on the roadway made her realize how hard this journey has been for Joseph as well. He had to leave his business and trade and become a father to a child he knew was not his own. She thought she had loved him before, and perhaps in a juvenile way, she had. But now she loved him not only as her betrothed, but loved him for being a man who heard and followed his God.

Joseph kept glancing back at Mary as he waited his turn in line. It was inconvenient to have to journey across the country to register for this census, and now having to wait in the hot sun was exasperating. He had brought whatever documentation he could: the names of his fathers to the fourth generation, and the record of his attendance at synagogue school. No doubt the census was for the purpose of taxing them even heavier, and everyone blamed Herod for using the population as his pawns to advance his prestige at Rome.

It was now the ninth hour and it looked like it could be another hour before Joseph would have his turn at the table. He could hear the gruffness of the Romans as they supervised the procedure. Most could not speak either Hebrew or Aramaic, so they had enlisted guards and officials from Herod's troops to do the documentation. They barked orders as needed and seemed to mock the peasants as they presented themselves. This census was not going to improve the relations between the population and Herod, perhaps even making things worse.

Joseph glanced anxiously towards where he had left Mary just before it was his turn at the table. He couldn't see where she was, although the donkey was still tied up where he left it. *She must have gone to get a drink or to refresh herself,* he thought. There was no way he was going to lose his place in the line now to find out for sure. She would take care of herself, he reasoned, and soon they would be leaving anyways.

Finally it was his turn. The questions were routine enough.

"Where were you born?"

"Nazareth."

"What is your age?"

"Twenty."

"Who was your father?"

"Jacob."

"And his father?"

"Matthan."

"And his father?"

"Eleazar. A lineage going back all the way to King David."

"What is your trade?"

"Carpenter."

"Do you own land?"

"No."

"Are you married?"

Joseph hesitated only a moment. "No."

"Do you have children?"

Joseph hesitated again. "No."

That was the end of the questions. Joseph waited to be handed his scrap of parchment etched with Roman numerals indicating his class and sealed with a mark to signify its authenticity. He was instructed to keep this safe since it would be the basis of any of his dealings with the authorities in the future. He was told he was free to go and amidst disparaging looks from the Roman soldiers he left the tent to find Mary.

She was nowhere to be found. He untied the donkey and led it around with him as he searched for her. First around the village well which was now crowded with people filling pitchers for the evening meal and the night to come. Next, he looked down the nearby alleys and streets. He had to resort to asking other women if they had seen Mary, most of whom would not even answer a man brash enough to talk to a woman he did not know.

Finally he found her, leaning against a wall down one of the alleys leading away from the village centre.

"Mary, are you all right?" Joseph quickly loosened a bundle from the donkey and positioned it behind her back. "Why did you leave the place where you were waiting?"

"You were gone a long time and the sun moved around so I had no shade," Mary explained. "Then I felt ill so I went down this alley in case I was sick."

"But you're all right now, aren't you?" Joseph encouraged her.

"I wasn't sick," Mary confessed. "But I am not all right. I am with child."

"I know that," Joseph reminded her. "And soon you will be at Elisabeth's."

"Yes, I will. But not tonight." Mary looked fully into Joseph's eyes to see the shock her words caused.

"What do you mean?" Joseph could not hide the frustration in his voice. "Why can't we make it there tonight? It is not much more than a few hours away, so you said."

"Because this child is coming now," Mary explained. "If not now, then very soon. I can hardly move let alone walk for hours."

"What?" Joseph said, clearly upset. "Are you sure?"

"Men!" Mary expressed her frustration with a sigh. "You know nothing about the ways of women."

"And I am not prepared to learn now!" Joseph protested.

"Then you must find us a place to spend the night," Mary pleaded. "We have to find a place where I can have this baby tonight, if that is what the Lord wills."

"It is certainly not what I will," Joseph grumbled under his breath. "Are you able to stay here while I find a place for us?" Joseph asked as his voice softened.

"No, you must not leave me alone again," Mary instructed him. "If you help me to walk, I will make it," she said with renewed confidence as she pushed herself away from the wall and leaned awkwardly on Joseph's shoulder. Putting her on the donkey in any fashion was not an option now, so Joseph wrapped the tether tightly around his arm so it could not loosen as he supported Mary with the other arm.

The streets were crowded as they left the security of the laneway to begin their search. The Romans had closed their registration table for the day and it seemed everyone was on the street either hawking goods for the evening meal or provisions for the travellers. Joseph jostled his way to the well and filled all their flasks with fresh water. The other women there gave him suspicion glances, and clucked to each other as they saw the young and now obviously pregnant girl in his company.

Walking away from the village centre, Joseph had opportunity to engage the street vendors, asking them where he might find a place to stay. Not one gave him any hope of finding a place. Everyone, it seemed, was already hosting more relatives than they could accommodate. Every vacant or abandoned place had been secured by the Romans for their use. Their only hope was the khan on their way out of the village.

"How are you doing, Mary?" Joseph asked as they maneuvered their way into a less crowded street.

"I'm managing, but I am not sure how much longer I can continue," Mary admitted.

"We can stop for a rest, if you wish," Joseph offered.

"We better not," Mary said between deep breaths. "I fear if I stop moving, I will not be able to get going again."

Worried by that comment, Joseph forged ahead, half carrying Mary as they left the side street and joined the busier road leading out of town. Many of the people would be travelling out of town and not be looking for a place to stay in Bethlehem as they were. There were several villages within an hour's walk away and he hoped they would all be heading to other locations to stay.

"I can't go any further," Mary gasped, as Joseph felt her relax more into his shoulder.

"You won't have to," Joseph reassured her. "We have arrived."

The khan at Bethlehem was like most of the khans in the hill country of Judea. The path into Bethlehem had to avoid a steep outcropping of rock, and the path became a road as the village grew. Eventually the village encompassed the outcropping and a home and outbuildings were built in front of the rock face, using the natural protection of the rocks as shelter for animals. An enterprising owner fitted the outbuildings as accommodation, and built sleeping quarters at advantageous locations along the rock face. There travellers could rest for the night and stay close to the animals that were travelling with them.

Joseph's heart sank as he approached the main house at the khan and heard the noise and bustle behind the buildings. *There must be a lot of people already here*, he mused. He didn't want to alarm Mary, so he let her rest by the remnants of an old well while he went to negotiate a place to stay. He took the donkey with him, thinking that the chance of an extra charge for an animal might help him secure a spot.

There was no negotiating with the keeper of this khan. He had no rooms left in the outbuildings, and all the sleeping lofts above the animal shelters were full. Joseph tried every negotiating tactic that Mary's brother Caleb had taught him from his travels, all to no avail. The only spot that was still unoccupied was one small animal shelter, so at least there was a place for the donkey to spend the night.

"I'll take it," Joseph heard himself saying.

As he led the donkey to its stall, he wondered how he would break the news to Mary. He had no place for her to stay. Their plan to register and then make their way to Elisabeth's the same day was not happening. And now he didn't even have an adequate place for her to spend the night to rest up enough to make to Elisabeth's in time for the child to be born.

I should have never brought her with me, he thought, scolding himself as he tied up the donkey. *I should have taken her straight to Elisabeth's and come to Bethlehem myself. This is not the way it was supposed to happen. She deserves better than this, after all she has been through already. Caleb will not be impressed with the way I am taking care of her, that is for sure.*

As Joseph approached Mary, she could see that he was troubled. "What's wrong, Joseph?"

"Everything." Joseph could not hide the despair in his voice. "I couldn't get anything for you. Only a spot for the donkey. I can try to make it comfortable for you there so you can rest enough to make it to Elisabeth's tomorrow and have the baby there."

"I won't make it to Elisabeth's to have the baby tomorrow,"

Mary panted out her words.

"What do you mean?" Joseph asked with concern.

Mary reached for his arm as she struggled to her feet.

"This baby is coming tonight!"

Chapter Twenty-Two
A Not So Silent Night

The sun dipped below the hills on the horizon and shadows quickly overcame the yard behind the khan. Fellow travellers had started a fire to ward off the coming chill of the night and to prepare evening meals. The smell of the smoke, the braying of the animals, and the chatter of the people congregating around the fire distracted everyone enough that they did not notice the girl heavy with child as she waddled through the camp.

Joseph tried to comprehend what Mary had just told him as he helped her walk towards the stall in the far corner of the khan. How could that baby come tonight? Who would help Mary with the delivery? Would she even know what to do? It was certain that he did not! Distracted by these thoughts, he offered no words of comfort to Mary as they reached their stall and he dutifully arranged their belongings along the stone wall in the pen.

For her part, Mary was in too much discomfort to pay attention to the others in the khan. Frantically, she tried to remember all the stages that Elizabeth had gone through when giving birth. By the regularity of the cramping she was now experiencing she knew it would not be long now. She arranged their blankets in a corner of the stall where she could sit and lean back against the rock wall, knowing she would need a solid place to push her back against.

As she settled into her nest, Mary noticed that Joseph was lost as to what to do. He had watched her arrange her place, and stared at her with a look of awkwardness, amazed at her calm demeanour.

"I'm going to be fine, Joseph," she reassured him. "This is much better than being on the road and not having any safe place at all."

"I can't believe you are okay with this," Joseph said. "I should have taken better care of you."

"You are taking care of me." Mary consoled him.

"I have no idea what to do next," Joseph admitted.

"I do," Mary said between winces of pain. "Find something to cover the opening to the stall so I have more privacy. And see if you can get some water heated up by the fire. I will need that."

"All right, that I can do," said Joseph, relieved that there was something he could focus on other than watching her in obvious discomfort.

Using a rope and the blanket from the donkey, Joseph arranged a crude curtain at the front of the stall. Excusing himself, he took one of the flasks to see if he could borrow a pot to heat up some water. He was happy to escape the drama unfolding in the stall for a few minutes, and was immediately guilt-ridden for feeling so. He had never been with Mary as man and wife, so how could he be there for the shockingly intimate experience of giving birth to a child? Surely Mary would understand; this was not something he planned on. He was accompanying her to Elisabeth's, where she and the other women would help with the birth, perhaps in a separate tent, while he and Zachariah swapped ancestral stories in the house, waiting for the news.

Mary wondered what was taking Joseph so long to return. Her birthing pains were not far apart now, and she grew increasingly nervous about being alone. What if the baby would not come and she struggled throughout the night? What if she passed out, and the baby lay there with no one to wrap it up from the chill of the night? What if the baby would not take to her breast, and there was no other woman to nurse the child? What if Joseph decided that this was all too much for him and did not return?

Her fears were interrupted by the irresistible urge to push. Mary squared her back against the wall. The urge to push subsided just long enough for her to catch her breath and see that Joseph had returned. She smiled weakly at him, amazed at how he could look bewildered and delighted at the same time.

"The cloths in the red blanket," Mary exhaled. "Have them ready."

"For what, Mary?" Joseph looked concerned as he put down the pot of water.

He reached for the cloths when Mary grunted as if moving a heavy boulder. She leaned against the rocks with a look of exhaustion on her face. Grabbing the cloths, Joseph rushed over to her and began to wipe her face with the cloths.

"Not me," she smiled weakly again. "The baby."

"The baby?" Joseph cried.

Nothing he had ever done as a carpenter or the visits he had made to the farms surrounding Nazareth had prepared him for the next moments. Ever so carefully he reached under the blankets that Mary had spread over her knees and felt for the baby, afraid to look.

He used the strips of cloth to shield the moist body from the roughness of his hands and carefully pulled the child out from between Mary's knees, placing the little boy on her lap. As the child gasped the night air, he began to cry, in loud short bursts, nothing that Joseph had ever heard before.

Mary was crying now, and between the two of them, Joseph was afraid the whole khan would hear. He continued to wrap the child, being careful not to damage the little cord still attached to the child. Suddenly he felt Mary's hands taking over from his, wrapping the child in the strips of cloth. Joseph leaned back and watched as she swiftly wrapped the baby in cloths as if she had been doing it her whole life, cooing softly to calm his cries. It was Joseph who was crying now, and embarrassed by his response and not sure what to do next, he turned away to get the warm water that he was sure Mary would be asking for next.

By the time he returned with the bowl of water, Mary had everything under control. She had severed the cord to the baby; Joseph didn't care to ask how. She held the baby close to her breast and continued to calm him with her cooing. As Joseph put the water within her reach, Mary nodded to a bundle of cloths with blood soaking through, and Joseph knew that was his next task.

As he left the stall to go to the fire, the activity at the khan had quieted down. Most had retired to their cots, and only a few of the older men sat around the fire, swapping ancestral stories. No one seemed to notice Joseph, and he was glad they had escaped anyone's attention. Hopefully Mary would have a quiet night and be rested up enough to finally make it to Elisabeth's. How she would do that with a newborn, he had no idea, but so far she seemed to know exactly what to do.

Joseph returned to the stall to find Mary half-asleep with the baby cradled peacefully in her arms. The moonlight wafted into their stall creating a soft glow that no lamp could achieve. *What a wonderful sight they are,* he thought. This beautiful young woman cuddling this tiny perfect child. In the roughest of surroundings, they were as beautiful as if they were in a palace. He kneeled beside them and used the warm water and a cloth, wiping Mary's forehead and smoothing her hair.

So it has all happened, Joseph thought, *just as the angel told Mary.* The virgin has conceived and brought forth a man child. And now he must do as his vision had instructed him. He would take Mary as his wife and raise this child as if it was his own. And he would have to do better than this. So far none of his plans had worked out, and he would have to do a better job of caring for his new family. How that would all work out, he did not know, and at this moment, he did not care.

"I thought I loved you all along," Joseph whispered so as not to wake Mary. "But that was nothing compared to the love I have for you tonight."

As if in response to his sentiments, Mary stirred and Joseph realized that maybe cradling the baby in her arms was uncomfortable for her and might not let her sleep peacefully. So he rose from his knees and took one of the blankets with him. He needed to find a safe place where the baby could lie without risk of falling or being stepped on. So he cleared out the depression in the rock where he had put the donkey's feed, and arranged the blanket inside the manger.

Carefully he lifted the child from Mary's arms and she immediately relaxed. *This baby weighs almost nothing,* Joseph thought as he cuddled the child to his chest. For some minutes he carried the baby, pacing back and forth across the stall, whispering his thoughts and prayers, telling the story of how he had fallen in love with his mother. Joseph apologized for having no better place to be born than an animal pen, and promised he would be sure to take better care of him from that moment on.

Gently he laid the baby in the blanket, and gathered the blanket around the cloths which were still wrapped around his tiny body. Joseph thought that maybe he should put something else around the child, but not knowing what that would be, he just made the blanket as snug as could be. He sat down beside this makeshift cradle with his back against the rocks, listening to every breath the baby took. *What a fine cradle I will make for you when we get home,* he thought. And while dreaming of the types of wood he would use and the way he would build it and polish it, Joseph fell asleep.

Chapter Twenty-Three
Shepherd Boys

Joseph didn't know if it was the stirring of the donkey or something else that woke him, but he jerked himself to his feet and peered into the moonlight. He glanced at the baby who still breathed regularly. Mary, although stirring, seemed to be asleep. He moved to the front of the pen, calming the donkey which was clearly agitated. The fire in the courtyard of the khan had gone out, and no one seemed to be around.

Then he heard them. Voices whispering in the dark, sounding like they were getting closer. Not the voices of men, but of boys. He stepped past the makeshift curtain he had made at the front of the stall to keep them away from Mary and the baby, whatever their intentions were. He had heard the stories of robberies in the night, and he was not going to let that happen to them.

The whispering voices grew closer and suddenly they stepped out of the shadows in front of Joseph. They were as they sounded, a group of boys who carried no weapons or purses, but one had a shepherd's staff, and another carried a small lamb under his arm. They stopped whispering as if on cue, and nearly bumped into each other as they stopped in front of Joseph, startled to see him.

"What are you doing here?" Joseph demanded. "Go back to your parents and leave us alone."

"We mean you no harm," the tallest of the boys said. "We are not staying at the khan. We are shepherds."

"Then go back to your sheepfold," Joseph said in as stern a voice as he could muster.

"We were with the sheep," another boy dared to explain to Joseph. "On the hillsides, just outside the village, when the most incredible thing happened."

"Joseph? Joseph? Who is there?" It was Mary, now awakened by the talking just outside the stall.

"No one, just some boys," Joseph reassured her.

"Do you have the baby with you?" Mary asked in an anxious voice.

Joseph could not talk or act fast enough. As soon as Mary had called out for the baby, the shepherd boys immediately started to talk all at once.

"Did you give birth to a baby today?"

"Is it a boy or a girl?"

"This could be the one the angel told us about!"

"I told you we should have come looking!"

"You have to name him Saviour!"

The shepherd with the small lamb under his arm darted behind Joseph and crawled under the curtain. Joseph tried to block him with his legs, but was not fast enough. By the time Joseph grabbed him they were both on their knees in front of the manger, the shepherd clinging to his lamb and Joseph's arms holding tightly to them both.

Joseph looked over to the corner where Mary reclined, thankful that she was still beneath her blankets and that her head was covered. Bad enough that these boys have intruded on their privacy, but it would have been worse if Mary was not suitably covered.

"I'm sorry, Mary," Joseph said as he loosened his grip on the boy to stand beside the manger between the boy and Mary. "I wanted you to have a good rest so I took the baby and laid him in the manger. Then I feel asleep watching over him and suddenly these shepherd boys wake everyone up and barge in here."

"Lying in a manger," the shepherd boy wondered aloud.

"Just like the angel said," said the taller boy as they had now all entered the stall.

"What did you say?" Joseph asked in a softer voice, realizing this group of shepherds posed no threat to his family.

"It's what the angel told us. We would find the baby wrapped in swaddling cloths, lying in a manger," he explained.

"That was a sign for us," continued another.

"A sign for what?" Joseph wanted to know, just as the baby began to cry. Joseph bundled the baby in the blanket and brought him to Mary who had pushed herself up from reclining and took the baby in her arms. Even in the dimness of the night, Joseph could see the look of amazement on the boys' faces as if they had never seen a baby before. No one dared to say anything, as if they didn't want to intrude on this sacred moment of mother and child.

It was Mary who spoke first, once she had soothed the child's cries. "Joseph, why don't you light a lamp so we can let these boys tell their story. Something happened tonight to bring them here, and we should hear what it is."

Joseph found the lamp and while lighting it the boys gathered in a group on the floor in front of the manger. As soon as the lamp lit up their faces Joseph could see that they were as young as he thought, and the boy with the lamb looked strangely familiar.

"If you try to not all talk at once, we will listen to your story,"

Joseph instructed them in as friendly a voice as he could under the circumstances.

Now it was Joseph and Mary whose faces were full of amazement as they listened to the shepherds' story. They didn't ask any questions or make any comments as the boys told what had happened. Mary smiled at them as they talked, treasuring every word they said, and Joseph only shook his head in wonder.

"We are shepherds who look after the temple flocks in the hills outside Bethlehem," the tallest boy explained.

"We look after the lambs of God," the boy holding the lamb offered.

"We are from two families who have worked together for generations," the tallest boy continued. "Most of them had fallen asleep and I was on the first watch. Suddenly there was this bright light coming from the sky, so bright it awoke everyone and it was brighter than daytime, so bright it was almost blinding. We were so scared we hid our faces in our cloaks and huddled together."

"Then when heard the voice of an angel," continued another boy. "It could only have been an angel, like the voice of a waterfall. He said that we were not to be afraid, that he was bringing us good tidings of great joy which shall be to all people. For unto us is born this day, in the city of David, a Saviour, who is Christ the Lord,"

"We are not sure what that means," interjected the boy with the lamb. "But maybe that is the name you are to give him."

"We were still completely scared," said another boy. "But the angel wasn't finished. He told us that there would be a sign for us. The baby would be wrapped in swaddling cloths, lying in a manger."

"Even we know that babies don't belong in a feeding pen," explained another. "So we figured that would be an unusual thing to find."

The tallest boy continued. "We thought we had seen everything. But then a whole host of angels joined the first one. It happened so fast we couldn't count how many there were, or what they looked like. Just glaring bright and loud like thunder. 'Glory to God in the Highest,' they proclaimed. 'And on earth, peace towards men of good will.'"

"We don't know what that means either," said the boy with the lamb. "We were too scared to ask."

"And then," continued another, "just as quickly as the light appeared, they were gone. And we were just as scared as ever in case they came back."

"So we waited for the longest while, and they didn't come back," the tall boy concluded. "We wondered why the angel would tell us what to look for if he didn't want us to look for the baby. So some of us came into the village to search, and those who were too scared stayed back with the sheep."

"We started searching all the animal pens and shelters that we knew of," explained a boy who hadn't yet spoken. "We knew if we told anyone what we were doing, they would think we were crazy, so we were glad that we were looking amongst animals, and not people's homes."

"And then I remembered about the khan," the boy with lamb shared with pride. "I knew there were lots of animal pens here, and maybe someone would have a baby with them."

It was only then that Joseph spoke. "We didn't have a baby, until tonight," Joseph admitted. "We were not planning to stay in Bethlehem at all, so this is all we could find at the last minute."

"Well, someone planned for you to be here," the tall boy concluded. "I don't know much about angels, but after tonight, one thing I know is that when they tell you something, it must be true."

"I'm beginning to learn that myself," Joseph agreed.

Mary didn't join the conversation as the boys and Joseph retold all that had happened that night. Distracted as they were by their storytelling, she took the opportunity to nurse the baby discreetly. They talked on through the night, and finally they bid goodbye and God's peace to them.

"Peace on earth," Mary thought she heard Joseph say as he stood outside the pen, lingering long after the shepherd boys were out of sight.

Joseph returned to the stall, looking at Mary with exasperation and exhilaration, something she was starting to recognize as his response to situations out of his control. He put out the lamp, and kneeling down, buried his head in the manger.

In the darkness, Mary could not tell if he was praying or weeping. Finally, she spoke. "You see, Joseph," her voice trembled as she realized what she was saying. "You had a good plan to get me to Elizabeth's for the birth of our son. But God had a different plan. You have not failed to take care of us. Just as the angels told us this child was to be born, the angels were watching over us right here in Bethlehem. And it is more wonderful than anything we could have ever imagined."

Chapter Twenty-Four
The Morning After

By the time the sun had completely risen over the hills, the khan was alive with women preparing morning meals, men packing up their animals for the day's journey, and children darting in and out amongst it all. The smell of the fires, the braying of the animals, and the shouts of the men all contributed to the atmosphere that resembled a feast day more than a travel day.

Joseph went to the well early to refill their flasks as Mary nursed the baby and tried to get some more sleep. He was unsure of what to expect from Mary, whether she would be able to travel or not. How he wished he had paid more attention to the families growing up around him in Nazareth so he would know more what to do for Mary.

But he didn't need to worry. When he returned to the stall, Mary was awake and the baby was snuggled in the blankets.

"You were a great help to me last night," Mary began. "I was so afraid of being alone, but you were there for me."

"I had no idea what to do," Joseph admitted. "And I still don't."

"Men never do," Mary assured him. "In regular circumstances, I would have midwives and other mothers with me, and you would be waiting in the house, arguing over what to name the child."

"There has been nothing regular about the birth of this child,"

Joseph said with that look of bewilderment. "And after that visit from the shepherds, I don't think anything will be regular anymore."

"That was the most wonderful experience that I will treasure in my heart forever," Mary agreed. "I thought I was all alone carrying this secret. And then Elizabeth knew, and while I was away an angel told you, and now, the angels tell shepherd boys to come and rejoice with us over the birth of this child."

"Mary," Joseph's voice hesitated. "It's all too much for me to handle. What am I supposed to do for this child, and for you?"

"You will know," Mary reassured him. "If God has done all this for us already, He will not abandon us now."

"Then we should continue on to Elisabeth's as we planned?" Joseph asked.

Mary did not hesitate to answer. "As soon as I am well enough to travel, we should," she said. "The child will need to be circumcised, and we have to give him a name."

"And we must have our wedding celebration," Joseph interrupted her.

"Not quite yet," Mary corrected him. "I must wait out my days of impurity."

"Your days?" Joseph really didn't know what she was talking about now.

"I have given birth to a man child," Mary explained. "So I am considered impure for 40 days to allow my body to recover. You are not allowed to touch me, and after the days are completed, we will offer a sacrifice to complete the ceremony."

"And then we will be formally married," Joseph insisted. "There has been, and probably will be, enough talk about us already. I will not let you return to Nazareth with a child unless you are my wife."

"And I will gladly be your wife, Joseph," Mary reassured him. "But now I need to rest and care for the baby."

"So you wish to stay here, in the stall for another day?" Joseph asked.

"I think we should, and then tomorrow I can make the journey to Elisabeth's," Mary suggested.

"All right then, I suppose it is better that you not move too much," Joseph agreed. "I will make arrangements with the khan master for another night, and then tomorrow we will leave."

When Joseph returned to their stall, he was greeted by an elderly woman who would not let him go in to Mary. Peering around her as she clucked on about the wonderful news of a man child being born, Joseph could see that he did not need to worry any more about Mary. She was surrounded by women attending to her and the child. Mary caught his eye and shrugged helplessly.

Apparently the news of the birth was common knowledge in the khan, Joseph thought, as the elderly woman instructed him to untie the donkey and take him to another stall. "Must have been those shepherd boys," he said aloud to the donkey as he fastened his lead to another stall. *How could a birth be any stranger than this?* he wondered, deciding to walk back into town to buy some provisions for the last leg of their journey. Hopefully Mary would be able to travel the next day. He was grateful for the help of the women, but they were strangers to them after all, and a short distance away was Elisabeth and the rest of her kinfolk who could look after Mary.

Joseph arrived at the market and bought some bread and dried fish. He paused at the lady who was offering linens for sale and fondled a bright blanket that he imagined the baby could be swaddled in for their journey. Not prepared to haggle over the price, he was ready to move on when half a dozen sheep tumbled out of the laneway, forcing Joseph to maneuver out of their way.

The shepherds followed in pursuit, shouting their commands and blocking the animals' path into the market lanes.

"I know you!" one of the boys pointed at Joseph who was trapped between the sheep and the wall of a shop.

"You had a baby born in the khan last night," another blurted out. "And we have been telling everyone about the angels and everything."

Joseph might have recognized the boys from the night before, but with all that happened and the dim light in the stall, he couldn't be sure. But there was no denying that they recognized Joseph. "Yes, we had a baby boy last night, as you say," Joseph beckoned one boy over to talk more privately. "But don't you think that it is a very private matter, and shouldn't be broadcast in the streets?"

"I suppose that is true most of the time," the boy agreed. "But when angels come to tell you about it, it is just too exciting to keep quiet. So we've been telling everyone! Hope you don't mind!"

With that, the shepherd ran off after the sheep as the other boys called for his help. *Great!* Joseph thought, as he hurried out of the market corridor before attracting any more attention. *Soon the whole village will know, and we will never escape to Elisabeth's. We will have to leave early tomorrow morning,* he planned, *before anyone shows up at the stall. Assuming those women let us have the night to ourselves,* Joseph mused as he returned to the khan.

Travellers were now leaving to continue on their journey, and many congratulated Joseph on the birth of the boy as Joseph returned to the khan. There were only two women attending to Mary when he checked up on her. Neither would let him near her, although they did bring the baby for Joseph to see. Swaddled up with only his sleeping face peering out, the baby was smaller than Joseph imagined a baby should be. Wispy black hair and puckered lips reminded him of Mary. Hopefully the child would be as beautiful as Mary, and not rugged looking like himself.

Joseph monitored the activity at the birthing stall throughout the rest of the day. Women came and went, bringing water, food and blankets, and leaving with what seemed like more than they brought in. At the time of the evening meal, they brought Joseph food as well. While he ate, the women gave him all kinds of instructions surrounding what he was to do for Mary and the child. Mary must have told them of the journey that she had yet to make to Elisabeth's. They cautioned him about allowing Mary to walk or sit for too long a time, and how he had to let her rest and nurse the child. They brought him the baby again, and showed him how to hold him while sitting, and how to carry him while walking. Joseph had no idea how complicated this could all be, and sometimes felt as if they were scolding him as much as they were instructing him.

Finally, as the shadows lengthened across the courtyard of the khan, the women left the stall where Mary had been all day, and motioned that Joseph could at last join her for the night.

Once inside the stall, he could see that Mary rested with her back against the rocks, softened by the blankets he had seen the women carry in. The baby was crying on her lap, and as Joseph picked him up, she smiled weakly.

"How are you doing, Mary?" he asked her as he cuddled the baby close to his face.

"I am sore, but otherwise just feeling very tired," Mary admitted. "Those women came out of nowhere to help, and that was great, but exhausting at the same time."

"Not quite out of nowhere," Joseph corrected her. "It was those shepherd boys who came last night. They've been telling everyone they can about the angels and you and the baby."

"Then maybe we should leave in the morning," Mary suggested. "Before we draw any more attention to ourselves."

"Or before well-meaning women keep me away for another whole day," Joseph agreed. The baby had stopped crying and Joseph eased him onto his chest as he too leaned back against the rock.

"If you can hold him Joseph," Mary said, "I will try to sleep until he needs to be fed again,"

"Of course, Mary," Joseph said. "I am used to handling rough blocks of wood, so I hope I am not too rough with him." Joseph shifted his position as the baby stretched. He looked over at Mary, expecting a response but she was already sleeping, or appeared to be. So Joseph laid in the dark stall, not wishing to disturb his sleeping family by lighting a lamp, thinking of how far he had come down this road, and where that road would now lead.

Chapter Twenty-Five

In the House of Zechariah

It was the third time Joseph had wrapped the baby in a new blanket and given him to Mary to be nursed. Each time, he had taken the baby back to the manger, hoping it would give Mary a chance to sleep. How much either of them slept that night didn't really matter. By the end of the third feeding, the animals were stirring restlessly as always before the break of dawn. They decided they would pack up and leave as soon as there was enough light to travel.

Because it was their final travel day, Joseph had traded or given away most of their cooking equipment and other supplies to lessen the load on the donkey. There would be more room and ability to carry Mary and the baby. As it was, with the extra blankets that they were given yesterday, Joseph would have to carry two packs himself.

They used the dim light of dawn to leave the khan without attracting attention to themselves. They were less than an hour on the road with the houses of Bethlehem now gleaming in the morning sun behind them, when Mary had to stop to rest. Joseph took the opportunity to water the donkey in a nearby ditch. This was going to take some getting used to, having a family to care for. But he was committed to them and was sure he would grow to love the baby as much as he did Mary.

By the time he rejoined Mary, she was gently rubbing the baby's back. She wrapped him up in the blankets and handed him to Joseph so she could position herself on the donkey. While he held the child, it occurred to him that he would not have to wait until the day of circumcision to name the child. He was sure that in his dream he was told that he was to name the child Yeshua.

"Yeshua," he said softly as he handed to child to Mary's outstretched arms.

"What did you say, Joseph?" Mary inquired.

"Yeshua," Joseph said proudly. "That is the name I was told in my dream to name your child."

"Our child, Joseph" Mary corrected him. "You have been chosen as much as me. This is a journey I would not want to be on alone."

"We are definitely not alone." Joseph assured her. "We were planning to be alone with Elisabeth by your side, and instead half the shepherd boys and women of Bethlehem were involved."

"That was so amazing!" Mary agreed. "Why would angels tell shepherd boys about the baby being born? I wonder what it all means?"

"It must have really happened, as fantastic as it sounds," Joseph offered as he picked up his packs. "There is no way a bunch of boys out in the fields at night would wander into town looking for a baby!"

With that, they started off again, Joseph leading the donkey along the road, trying to avoid the rougher sections. They travelled in silence for another hour, each lost in their thoughts of all that had happened. It was the cry of the baby that prompted Joseph to stop for another break. By then, they had left the sparsely treed rocky slopes of middle Judea and were in the rolling fertile hills that surrounded

The Love of Mary

the plateau of Jerusalem. Tying the donkey to a tree, he helped Mary down to rest in the shade.

"How much further do we have to go?" Joseph wanted to know.

Mary gave the baby to Joseph so she could arrange Joseph's packs into a makeshift table to change the baby's blankets. Looking up, she studied the hills rising to the west in front of them. "I'm sure it will be not much more than an hour or two," Mary replied. "At least I hope so."

"Are you able to go another hour?" Joseph asked as he handed the baby back to Mary.

"If I nurse the child here, and then you hold him so I can rest for a little while," Mary suggested, "I'll be fine."

"Okay. You just have to let me know. I have no idea what kind of discomfort or pain you are in, so you have to let me know" Joseph told her as he arranged some blankets for Mary to lie on.

There were no other travellers on the road so Joseph felt comfortable leaving Mary alone to walk around with the baby. "You shall call his name Yeshua, for he will save his people from their sins," Joseph whispered into the baby's ear the words the shepherd had told him in his dream months ago. And as he cradled the baby, walking among the rocks and shrubs, he wondered if the angel that the shepherd boys had talked about was the same angel that appeared to Mary. And maybe the shepherd in his dream was actually an angel as well.

And now he helped this little angel with no idea what to do next. They didn't make it to Zechariah and Elisabeth's for the birth, but perhaps going there now will help them sort out what to do next. The boy would have to be circumcised, and his name announced. Mary would have to offer a sacrifice for the man child at the temple, and they were not yet married. *I will be glad for the old priest's advice on all these matters,* Joseph thought as he returned to find Mary sitting up and anxious to finish their journey.

With Mary positioned on the donkey again, Joseph continued to carry the child as they started back on the road. The road was steeper now as they continued to climb the hills that formed the plateau around Jerusalem. From the crests of the hills, they could catch glimpses of Ain Karim in the distance. Joseph was not sure, as he had never been there before, but Mary seemed to know her way, and just the sight of their destination gave them new energy.

By some miracle, the baby remained sleeping as Joseph cradled him in one arm, while managing one bundle over his shoulder, and another in his other arm. This did not escape the notice of Mary, who wondered how he was so capable on his first days as a father.

"It's the fourth house we pass going down this hill," Mary announced as they reached the final hill before the village. Preparing herself to greet her kin, Mary dismounted the donkey and took the baby from Joseph. Joseph thankfully transferred his burdens to the donkey and tried to get the beast to keep up with Mary who was now almost running down the narrow, stony road.

Joseph was apprehensive about the reception they would receive, but he didn't need to worry. Elisabeth came darting out of the house before Mary even reached the path to the door, as if she knew when Mary was arriving. When she realized that Mary was carrying the baby, she cried out so loudly it startled the donkey. And it must have startled Zechariah as well, as he appeared at the front door to see what all the commotion was about. Snuggled in the old man's arms was another miracle baby: John, now six months old.

Zechariah passed John to Elisabeth as her and Mary entered the house, both talking so excitedly at the same time it was impossible for the men to understand what they were saying.

"Shalom, Joseph," Zechariah offered. "I see the Lord has been with you," he said as he took the donkey and led it to the animal shelter behind the house.

"Verily, the Lord has helped us," Joseph agreed.

Once the donkey had been watered and secured, Zechariah helped Joseph with their bundles and joined the women in the house. The next hours were spent sharing their stories of the last months and days. There was talk of angels and dreams and not being able to talk and of shepherds and believing all that the Lord had revealed to them. The talking never stopped as the evening meal was prepared and eaten, and then as the sleeping arrangements were made for Mary and the baby and for Joseph.

Mary had told Joseph the story of Zechariah and Elisabeth and John, but hearing it from their own mouths, and holding the baby promised to them was almost too much for him to comprehend. Before they retired for the night, Joseph finally blurted out. "If I were not holding your baby tonight, I would have a hard time believing your story."

"If I were not here holding your baby boy," Zechariah's eyes smiled as he continued, "I definitely would not believe *your* story."

"Mary has had this miracle baby, and we are not yet married, so what am I supposed to do now?" Joseph pleaded.

Zechariah walked over and placed both of his hands on Joseph's shoulders. "I have not the slightest idea," he said.

Joseph sighed deeply and tried to raise his arms in frustration, but the old priest would not loosen his grip.

"But the Lord does," Zachariah continued. "And He will guide your path."

Chapter Twenty-Six
The Eighth Day

Life at Zechariah and Elisabeth's home was simple and humble. As a priest, he was only on duty at the temple in Jerusalem two weeks of the year. The rest of the time he spent at home tending their small plot of land for fresh food. As an older man, gone were the days of travelling to Bethlehem to source temple sheep. He was called upon to serve the local people with advice and religious rituals that didn't require a performance at the temple. His time at home was mingled with weddings, the observance of Feast Days, overseeing the local synagogue, the resolution of disputes, and circumcision.

And so the arrangements were made for Mary's baby to be circumcised on the eighth day, upon which his name would be revealed. Joseph hoped to keep it as private an affair as possible, not wanting the relationship between him and Mary to be put under too much scrutiny. All the circumstances surrounding the naming of John did not help towards that end.

For her part, Mary was an attentive and nurturing mother. The baby settled into a nursing and sleeping schedule that allowed her enough time to rest and not interfere with Elisabeth's care of John. Joseph helped Zechariah with his chores and accompanied him on

The Love of Mary

his visits to the townsfolk, who were only too happy to have a real carpenter around to help with building and repairs. Joseph was willing to help, realizing that whatever little money he could make during their stay would help to replenish his dwindling purse. Many of the poorer folk could not pay at all, but would offer bread or vegetables or eggs, which Joseph accepted, knowing that it would help Elisabeth set a table for four every evening.

Hardly an evening went by that they didn't retell their stories and experiences surrounding the birth of the boys. Mary was the most contemplative of them all, sometimes listening, but lost in her own thoughts and emotions. By the end of the week, Joseph felt like he was getting to know Zechariah and Elisabeth fairly well, and could see his role fitting into this family.

On the eighth day, Elisabeth's kin and friends gathered at the house, much the same people who were there for the naming of John. Most of them remembered Mary being there, and were so focused on the new baby she had brought with her this time, that they paid little attention to the exact status of Joseph. They just assumed they were husband and wife and no inquiries were made to the contrary.

Much of the talk was about the amazing sight before them: an aging Elisabeth, old enough to be a grandmother, with her baby; and young Mary, barely out of girlhood, with her newborn. The men noticed it as well, but Zechariah had already suffered for making remarks about being too old, so he had learned to keep silent. Joseph was learning from his experience.

The ceremony itself was simple enough. A hymn sung by all who could, a prayer by the priest, and the cry of the baby as the knife did its work. Another prayer by the priest, and then it was Joseph's turn.

"His name shall be called Yeshua," he announced with all the authority he could muster. As he said the words, all the visuals of his dream flooded back and almost overwhelmed him. What was he to do with this boy who was destined to save his people from their sins, as he was told? How was he supposed to make that happen?

Thankfully, Zechariah spoke up before anyone noticed the anxiousness on Joseph's face. "Yeshua means The Lord who saves. A wonderful promise to us all."

With that, Zechariah led in another prayer. Once he was done, there were a few questions about why that name, as there was at the naming of John, but Elisabeth took her liberties and explained that Joseph and his family hail from Galilee and he was told that was to be the name, so there would be no further discussion on the matter. She conveniently left out the part that it was an angel that told him what the name should be. But the guests were satisfied with that, and turned their attention to Mary who was soothing Yeshua and the food that was now available.

Later in the evening, after all the guests had gone and the boys were sleeping, Joseph had some time to talk with Mary. With all the busyness of the last week with tending to the baby and preparing for the ceremony, they had talked very little. After spending the days travelling to and from Bethlehem together and only having each other for conversation and support, they had been distracted from each other by the ongoing dialogue with Zechariah and Elisabeth.

They talked long into the evening after their hosts had gone to bed, reviewing all their feelings about the events of the day and the journey that had led them here. Joseph felt that he wanted to stay by her side all night long, he was feeling so connected to her, but Yeshua started to stir for another feeding, and he knew his time with

Mary was up for now. As Joseph left, he resolved that he would make this marriage happen sooner, rather than later, and he would be talking to Zechariah about that really soon.

"Yeshua," Mary cooed as she picked up her baby. "That's a beautiful name, is it not, Joseph?"

"It is," he agreed, and he walked back and kissed the child on the forehead.

Chapter Twenty-Seven

A Building Plan

"How can this be done?" Zechariah wanted to know as he walked into town with Joseph the next day.

"I don't know exactly." Joseph hesitated. "But it must be done, for the sake of Mary and her reputation, and for the child."

"And what of you and your family back in Nazareth?" was Zechariah's next objection.

"They know we were betrothed, and that she would accompany me to Bethlehem. By the time we left, no one knew she was with child. If we return as a married couple with a child, it is really only the family I work with that would give me any grief, and I can deal with them."

"And what of Mary's kin?" was the next inquiry.

"There is really only her brother Caleb that Mary would insist must be here for the wedding. We all grew up together, and it is Caleb who approved our betrothal and helped convince me to go through with it once Mary knew she was with child."

"And a visit from an angel wasn't enough to persuade you?" Zechariah teased him. "Mine left me speechless!"

"Mine too!" Joseph agreed. "But Caleb was the one who told me in the first place and started the whole process. This is going to be a small, quiet affair, and Mary's brother just has to be here."

They were now on the dusty streets of the small town as Zechariah made his way to the doorway of a widow where he left his delivery of bread. In all the small towns of Judea it was the local priest who was also the caregiver of the sick and elderly and arranged the distribution of alms and foodstuffs to the needy. It was not a task Zechariah took lightly, and would often do without to make sure all the needs were met. Mary had told Joseph about their good works, and he was glad to see it in action.

A few more stops to check on some more elderly and one sick boy, and they were on their way back home up the hills and the conversation picked up again.

"Caleb knew Mary was planning to give birth here under the care of Elisabeth," Joseph explained.

"That would have been an excellent plan," Zechariah offered.

"It was," Joseph agreed. "But we didn't get here in time, and poor Mary had to deliver her firstborn in a khan, of all places. And then a bunch of shepherd boys find out and tell who knows how many people all around the village. It is a good thing we were strangers there and no one else will find out about the miserable beginning I gave to Mary and her first child."

"Don't be too hard on yourself," Zechariah consoled him. "If I got the story right, not only did an angel tell you to take Mary as your wife, but angels told the shepherds boy where you were the night little Yeshua was born."

"What's your point?" Joseph was not to be consoled.

"It means that the Lord Jehovah chose you to be the father of this child," Zechariah schooled him. "Because he trusted your love for Mary. And if His angels were watching over you, then you have nothing to fear. It is better to be spending the night in an animal shelter with angels watching over you, than to be born in the king's palace without God's favour."

"I get what you are saying," Joseph agreed. "But the less people who know about the trouble I put Mary through, the better. I suppose Mary will tell Caleb all about it, and I hope that does not make him think me an inadequate husband."

"It won't, I am sure," Zechariah reassured him. "When did you want the wedding to happen?

"As soon as possible!" Joseph's voice betrayed his excitement. "I can hardly wait!"

"But for some things you will have to wait," Zechariah cautioned. "Mary is still impure for another month, and then you will have to offer the redemption price for her man child, and an offering for her purification."

"I know it," Joseph agreed, but his enthusiasm was not dampened. "I just have to give her as much of a marriage ceremony as I can. She deserves that much at least."

They had arrived home, and the evening meal was already on the table. There was no more talk of wedding plans, as this was not something you would discuss with the women. Eventually the conversation turned to when Joseph and Mary should return to Nazareth. Joseph's purse was almost empty, and so he thought they should leave soon after the ceremony in the temple.

"And where will you live?" Elisabeth wanted to know.

"Caleb has said that we could live with him until I could get a place of our own ready," Joseph offered. "He is planning to sell the house and move to Jerusalem, so we would not stay there for very long."

"And there will be room for little Yeshua there?" Elisabeth was persistent.

"As much as there is here, that is for sure," replied Joseph, trying not to sound ungrateful.

Mary was not as anxious to leave the house of Elisabeth and Zechariah as Joseph was. She felt safe here. For three months, it had been her refuge and source of wise counsel from Elisabeth. She was as fond of the old priest as she was when she was a child, and treasured the memories he was writing down for her. And since the birth of Yeshsua in Bethlehem, it was as if she had brought him home. As much as she knew Joseph thought it was time for them to go, she was reluctant to do so.

"We will be most comfortable there," Mary jumped into the conversation to rescue Joseph. "You needn't worry about us, Elisabeth. After all we have been through, setting up a home with a baby will be the least of our troubles."

"You are probably right about that," Zechariah agreed, looking up from his tablets. "Your biggest trouble will be that people talk."

"Our story," Mary disagreed, "will stay as our story. Not a topic for discussion at the marketplace."

"Your story will become the talk of the town," Elisabeth cautioned. "When you show up with a baby less than two months after you left to get married."

This was not something Joseph had spent a lot of time considering. He had gone to great lengths to maintain Mary's dignity through all of this. Having to explain everything to the people in Nazareth would be much more difficult than the encounters they had with shepherds and people they would never see again.

"You are welcome to stay in the house of Zechariah as long as you wish," Zechariah offered.

"And think of the memories we will have of little John and Yeshua growing up together," Elizabeth added.

"And think how crowded it will get as they get bigger," Joseph countered.

"Then we should hire a carpenter to put another room on the house," Zechariah teased. "I wonder where we could find one we could afford?"

That was all the challenge Joseph needed. Although he had abandoned his plans to build a house for Mary in Nazareth, building was in his blood. Even if they only stayed for a short while, the addition of a room on the house would be a great way to repay Zechariah and Elisabeth for all their kindness to them. John would need a room of his own one day, after all.

"What are you thinking, Joseph?" Mary wanted to know.

Joseph did not dare to reveal all he was thinking. The new room would not only be for raising Yeshua, but would be the wedding chamber where they would spend their wedding night together if he could get it ready in time.

"I am thinking that what Elisabeth says is true," he replied after a long pause. "There is really no reason for us to return to Nazareth right away. And the longer we stay away, the less you have to explain whenever we do go back."

"Joseph?" Mary questioned, as she reached out for his hand. "Are you sure?"

"After all we have been through," Joseph began, "How can I be sure of anything? But this seems like the best plan for you and baby Yeshua."

"The best plan for us," Mary corrected him, as she squeezed his hand.

Chapter Twenty-Eight
Rituals

Joseph began building right away. He took the stones out of the bottom of the window facing the garden, turning it into a doorway for the new room. Using these stones and others gathered from around the property, he started to build the walls. When he ran out of stones on Zechariah's property, he gathered rocks from neighbours in exchange for his labour on their own projects.

He used many of the ideas he had dreamed about for their home in Nazareth. He designed it with a door to the outside garden so it would feel like they were entering their own home. The stone wall extended past the door to form a little courtyard for privacy.

He acquired beams for the roof from older buildings in the village that were too dilapidated to repair. The beams extended past the outside wall to continue the roof over the courtyard. Here the babies could be outside in the breeze, but out of the sun.

Gathering the sheaves of chaff from the last harvest, he weaved them together to make tiles for the roof. He completed all these things without spending any money from his dwindling purse.

Mary's ritual time was almost up, and they needed to plan the trip to Jerusalem. Joseph accompanied Zechariah on one of his errands into town so he could talk about their trip and his wedding plans away from the women.

"You have certainly done a lot of work on your room," Zechariah complimented him.

"I need to get it finished," Joseph said. "Then, when we return from Jerusalem, the wedding can happen as soon as Caleb arrives."

"When we go to the temple, you will have to offer a lamb for a burnt offering, and a turtledove or a pigeon as a sin offering for Mary," Zechariah informed him.

"Whatever you say," Joseph said. "I know very little about temple rituals."

"Then you probably do not know that you also must have five shekels as the price of redemption for your firstborn son," Zechariah reminded him.

After all we have been through, now I have to pay a temple price for Mary to have a son? Joseph thought, but did not dare say it out loud.

"I will most certainly be out of money by then," Joseph calculated. "How much do lambs cost anyways?"

"More than you or I both have with the boys to look after," Zechariah lamented. "But the Law does allow those who cannot afford a lamb to bring an extra bird for the burnt offering."

"That's the answer!" Joseph exclaimed. "I don't have to find the money to buy a lamb. I'll build a snare and catch a couple pigeons."

Zechariah agreed. "Many poor people in these hills snare birds and bring them to the temple for sacrifice. I sacrifice more birds than lambs in years of hardship. But I think the turtledove is an easier catch."

"Then turtledoves it will be," Joseph confirmed. "And as soon as

Caleb arrives, the wedding ceremony can happen?" Joseph wanted to know.

"As long as we give Mary enough time to prepare herself," Zechariah cautioned. "Once we return from Jerusalem, we will tell her that the bridegroom is coming, and she should prepare herself. During those days, you should live away from the house."

"And stay away from Yeshua as well?" Joseph asked.

"Yes," Zechariah confirmed. "But it will only be for two or three days. That is why we should not say anything until Caleb arrives."

"All right," Joseph agreed. "Until he comes, I will try to get the room finished."

"We won't be able to include all the traditions of a normal wedding," Zechariah cautioned. "But we will make it as special as we can."

"That is all I ask," Joseph said. "Mary is missing out on so much that a bride should have. I want her to at least have a wedding ceremony."

Joseph and the aging priest were quiet and reflective on the way home. Just before they reached the house, Joseph had one more question. "An angel told you about the birth of John, right?" Joseph asked.

"That's right," Zechariah confirmed. "Just like you."

"And did the angel tell you what you were supposed to do?" Joseph asked. "As in how you were to raise him and prepare him for whatever God wanted him to do?"

"Only that he was not to drink wine or strong drink," Zechariah admitted.

"I got no instructions, other than what his name was to be," Joseph lamented. "What I am supposed to do? I can plan how to take care of Mary, but how am I supposed to raise Yeshua? I may never have enough money to send him to school. I may not even be able to take him to Jerusalem once a year."

"Joseph!" Zechariah assured him. "As much as Jehovah chose Mary to give birth to this child, he chose you to be the father. The Lord Jehovah trusts you to do the right thing. And if an angel guided you once, He can send an angel to guide you again."

"I think once was quite enough!" Joseph said with conviction.

Mary saw their approach and opened the door to greet them, ending the conversation abruptly. She cradled Yeshua in her arms and offered the sleeping bundle to Joseph. It was late in the day so Joseph strolled about the garden rocking him gently and voicing all his questions about what their life would be like here.

As the sun lowered over the hills in a blaze of red and orange, Joseph heard the birds. Then he saw them, two turtledoves perched on end of the stone wall of the new room. He laughed at his doubts, striding confidently back to the house, anxious to tell Mary of all that was filling his heart.

Chapter Twenty-Nine

Sacrifice

Joseph tried four different types of snares before he caught the turtledoves that had mocked him from the stone fence. In that time Zechariah had made one journey to Jerusalem and brought back a borrowed cage in which to keep them. The final days of Mary's purification drew near, and so the plans to go to the temple were finalized. Elisabeth would stay at home with John, and Zechariah would accompany Mary and Joseph to help them navigate the temple rituals.

They left two days before the Sabbath in case they were delayed for any reason, so they would not have to travel on the Sabbath day. As they walked along, Joseph was not sure who was slowing down the pace more: Mary and Yeshua, or old Zechariah. Not only were there frequent stops for rest, but it seemed like everyone who passed by wanted to talk to the priest or look at the baby. Their two hour walk stretched into three by the time they reached the streets of Jerusalem, and the temple was on the hill at the other side of the city.

If Joseph thought the travel in the country was slow, it became a crawl in the city. The streets were crowded and noisy, busier than when he and Mary were there just weeks ago. He wondered why Caleb would ever want to live here. King Herod had built a palace that towered on a hill over the temple, and that landmark was their focus as they meandered the streets. At least Zechariah knew which paths to take, and Joseph was glad he had come along.

Joseph carried Yeshua much of the way, especially since they had reached the crowded streets of the city. As the temple came into view, Mary thought it best to find a quiet alley and nurse Yeshua there so she would not have to do it at the temple. When it came time to sacrifice, she would have to wait in the court of women alone while the men went further inside the temple to offer their sacrifice. There would be no opportunity for privacy at that point. Zechariah knew the corner of a building she could use, and Joseph was again glad he had come along.

Built by the exiles who had returned from Persian captivity four hundred years before, the temple was an imposing structure, but it was not the golden gilded temple that Solomon built. That had been destroyed in wars and stripped of its treasures. Still, it was magnificent with its columns and steps and inner courts. Joseph was just as interested in the architecture as he was the religious rites that took place inside.

As they approached the temple steps, they avoided the tables of merchants selling linens and sandals and jewelry and foodstuffs of every sort. At the steps were the merchants selling lambs, pigeons, and turtledoves for sacrifice. The prices they cried out were so ridiculously high that Joseph wondered if he could quit carpentry and go into the bird business.

Once up the steps and into the court of women it was quieter, but just as crowded. They worked their way through the crowds of women and children, approaching the trumpet-shaped chest where the shekels for the redemption of the boy were to be deposited. Mary's coins had just dropped into the chest when an aged man grasped Joseph by the shoulders as if he had been waiting there for him.

Thinking this must be someone Zechariah knew, Joseph looked over to Zechariah expecting an introduction but Zechariah looked as astonished as Joseph felt.

The old man held on to Joseph's coat but his gaze had left Joseph's eyes and were fixed upon little Yeshsua cradled in Mary's arms.

"Shalom," Joseph offered tentatively, hoping to break the awkwardness of the moment.

"Lord, now let your servant depart in peace, according to your Word," the old man finally blurted out in a cracking voice suited to his age.

Without warning, he reached for little Yeshua, and Mary was so surprised she made no resistance.

"For my eyes have seen the salvation of Lord God Jehovah," he continued. "Which you have prepared before for the people. A light for the Gentiles, and the glory of your people Israel."

They were all too astonished to speak. Joseph moved closer to the aged man to retrieve Yeshua, but before he could, the man bent over and gave the baby back to Mary. He wasn't finished speaking.

"Behold, this child is set for the fall and rising again of many in Israel; and for a sign which shall be spoken against," he continued, focusing on Mary. "Yes, a sword shall pierce through your own soul also, that the thoughts of many hearts may be revealed."

Not even Zechariah knew how to react to this aged man and his strange prophecies. Joseph moved to Mary's side as if to help her comprehend all that had just happened.

"His name is Yeshua," Mary offered.

"Of course, it should be," the old man answered and turned to go. Zechariah grasped his arm and helped him on his way, and Joseph could hear them talking as they left.

"Mary, are you all right?" Joseph wanted to know. "That was a really strange way to talk about a baby!"

"I know," Mary agreed. "I don't know how we are supposed to receive all of this. Even amongst all these people, somehow we are singled out and told so many things we don't understand."

It was several minutes before Zechariah returned, alone and shaking his head. "I can't say I recognize him, although I am sure I have seen him at the temple here before," Zechariah began. "His name is Simeon and he has an amazing story. He has been praying for years for the deliverance of our people Israel, and is convinced that Jehovah has revealed to him that he would not die until he had seen the salvation of Israel."

"And what does that have to do with us?" Mary wanted to know.

"He believes that little Yeshua is the promised one, that would save the people from their sins," Zechariah offered.

"From their *what*?" Joseph was not sure he heard correctly.

"From their sins," Zechariah repeated. "It is a promise repeated through all our Law and Prophets."

"I thought that is what you said," Joseph affirmed. "That is the exact language the shepherd in my dream used. 'Call his name Yeshua for he shall save his people from their sins.'" Joseph moved closer to Mary. The strange way Simeon spoke about the baby and Mary made him uneasy.

"Mary," Zechariah instructed, "you are to go with the other women to the top of the stairs where you will be able to see and share in the sacrifice. When the hymn is done, we will come back and join you."

Mary could see the unwillingness in Joseph's eyes to leave her alone.

"Go ahead, I will be fine." Mary assured him.

Zechariah picked up the cage with the turtledoves and started up the steps. Joseph reluctantly left Mary and disappeared up the stairs into the inner court.

The court of sacrifice was a cacophony of noise, shouts, smells, and smoke. The bleating of sheep, the clucking of fowl of every sort, and the shouts of the priests as they performed their rituals all added to the confusion. Fortunately for Joseph, Zechariah was able to guide him and before long they were at the altar of sacrifice.

Joseph was glad Mary was not with them to witness the sacrifice. The priest removed the turtledoves from the cage and promptly broke their necks. Blood dripped onto the base of the altar. Then he put them on the altar that was already burning with carcasses of the sacrifices before theirs, an aroma that hung in Joseph's nostrils like a blanket. All the while the priest chanted and sang passages from the Torah, much of which Joseph did not recognize.

The priest finally proclaimed his blessing on Yeshua and they were able to leave. Little Yeshua seemed oblivious to it all and slept through the whole ceremony. How this cleansed Mary of her impurity Joseph did not understand. Zechariah's attempt to explain it to him as they jostled their way back through the crowd was lost on him, as he was focused on getting back to Mary and away from the crowds.

As they reached Mary, Joseph was relieved to see she was not alone. An elderly woman was keeping her company. "How was Yeshua?" Mary wanted to know as Joseph gave the baby back into her waiting arms.

"Good as could be," confirmed Joseph. "We are all finished now, and we can return home."

Suddenly the elderly woman interrupted. "So this is the child of promise!" she exclaimed, loud enough for all around them to hear. "The people that walked in darkness have seen a great light," she proclaimed. "For unto us a child is born, unto us a son is given: and the government shall be upon his shoulder: and his name shall be called Wonderful, Counsellor, The Mighty God, The everlasting Father, The Prince of Peace."

Joseph was startled to hear the invocation of peace again. That was the same language that the shepherd boys said the angels declared to them: "Peace on earth." How could he ever forget that! And how could all these be related?

Joseph searched Mary's face for her reaction. She looked just as dumbfounded as he felt, but quickly turned her attention to Yeshua.

Thankfully, the elderly woman left their company but was still proclaiming the mighty works of Jehovah to any would listen as she walked along.

"If we can leave now we can make it home without stopping for another feeding for the baby," Mary offered.

"And maybe without another interruption from people we don't even know," Joseph added.

"All right," Zechariah agreed. "You two start out. I want to return this birdcage to the vendors I borrowed it from. I will catch up with you on the road."

Agreeing, Mary and Joseph made their way through the crowds with Yeshua, trying not to attract any more attention than they already had. They were well on the road outside the city before either of them dared to untangle their thoughts about the day.

"Are you starting to notice that many of the things being told to us are somewhat similar?" Joseph asked.

"Somewhat?" Mary pushed back. "They are more than *somewhat* similar. When you and Zechariah were making sacrifice, that elderly woman approached me out of nowhere. Her first words to me were: "Blessed are you among women, and blessed is the fruit of your womb.""

"That is significant?" Joseph asked.

"Of course!" Mary chided him. "Those are the exact words that Elizabeth greeted me with when I showed up at her house before I even told her I was expecting!"

"Maybe that is a common greeting among women," Joseph wondered aloud.

"No, it is not," Mary informed him. "And it is certainly not the way you greet a total stranger.

"Did you find out who she was?" Joseph wanted to know.

"Her name was Anna," Mary began. "She became a widow after seven years, and has basically lived at the temple, praying and fasting for the last eighty-four years."

"She would be as old as Methuselah then," Joseph teased.

"Just about," Mary said, ignoring his jest. "But somehow she knew that we had given birth to a special child."

"Her, the old man Simeon, the shepherds," Joseph started to compile a list. "Elizabeth, and who knows who else? I thought we were keeping this all to ourselves. Another failed plan."

"When the Lord Jehovah sends angels to change your plans I would not call that a fail," Mary said firmly,

Before Joseph could object, Zechariah's voice called out to them to stop for a minute so he could catch up. They spent the rest of the way home trying to unravel all that had happened. Zechariah had no real answers other than a firm belief that as Jehovah had spoken to them through angels and dreams, it was entirely possible that Jehovah had spoken to Anna and Simeon. They had not just heard the incoherent ramblings of very aged, perhaps confused people, but the voice of Jehovah.

They finally reached the crest of the hill where they turned onto the path home. As if on cue, baby Yeshua started to fuss for another feeding when they started up the path to the house. Mary was glad for the chance to nurse. She was so tired from the journey to Jerusalem and back, and emotionally exhausted after all the events at the temple. She would be grateful for the time alone to reflect.

Chapter Thirty
A Wedding at Last

Mary fell asleep while nursing Yeshua, and Joseph had managed to join them in their sleeping quarters without waking either of them. Now the morning would be spent telling all that happened in Jerusalem. Elizabeth had to know it all in every detail. She was especially intrigued that the aged woman Anna had greeted Mary exactly as she had.

For his part, Zechariah wrote furiously all morning on his parchment, frequently stopping them to tell the story all over again so he could get it down word for word. Near the end of the morning he had run out of parchment and took to recording on the writing tablets he used when he had no voice.

Once they had exhausted all the details, Zechariah rose to make an announcement: "Behold, the bridegroom is coming, and all should be made ready."

Mary gasped. Joseph rose to leave, touching her hand as he did so. Other than passing the baby back and forth, that was the only touch they had shared since the birth of Yeshua. She realized in that moment how much she missed the touch of his hand.

Joseph went over to the wooden basket that Yeshua had inherited from John and kissed the baby on the forehead. He left the room and paused just long enough at the door to see Mary's dark eyes filling with tears.

They did not see each other again until the wedding night.

Mary was gaining her strength back as Yeshua had settled into a somewhat regular feeding pattern. She was grateful for the all the help Elisabeth had given and wondered how she would have managed on her own. With her wedding day now imminent, she was both thrilled and anxious. Thrilled that somehow after all these months of uncertainty she would have a normal life with the man she knew loved her deeply. Anxious that she did not know where this journey together would take them and how they were to raise this son given to them.

Mary was sure Joseph would not come for her until Caleb arrived, which could be any day now. Filled with uncertainty until now, she had not even started her wedding dress. She threw herself into the task now, and with help from Elisabeth sewed a beautiful dress and headpiece. Without raising suspicions, Elisabeth borrowed as much jewelry as she could to fasten to the veil.

Wedding nights were usually followed by days of feasting and merriment. While the women were not sewing or looking after the babies, they were preparing all the special dishes fit for a wedding. Elisabeth's plan was to invite her relatives for the days following the wedding to celebrate the babies and to visit with Caleb. That way, Mary and Joseph would experience the celebration of their wedding while avoiding any potential embarrassment.

Caleb finally arrived one day at noon. He had come to Jerusalem to register for the census, and, as promised, made the journey to the house of Zechariah.

His arrival overwhelmed Mary. Usually quiet and reflective, Mary took the whole afternoon to tell Caleb all that had happened since they left Nazareth: the journey, the stable, the shepherds, and their trip to the temple.

After the evening meal, Mary gave a plate of food for Caleb to take to Joseph, who had been staying out of sight, sleeping in the hills like a shepherd boy

"You two have had quite an adventure, I hear," Caleb declared as he offered the meal to Joseph. "Mary spent the whole afternoon going over every detail."

"That we have," Joseph agreed. "If you remember some months ago, I really didn't want to take Mary on this journey, but she insisted. It did not work out exactly as planned."

"And maybe it was better that it didn't work out according to plan," Caleb countered. "Come on, Joseph, you really had no idea what to expect! It sounds like the Lord Jehovah took over for you."

"Have you been talking to Zechariah?" Joseph asked.

"No, but if he speaks the same to you as me," Caleb continued, "then you know what we say: if two or three agree. Think about it! If angels are the ones announcing the birth of your child and not the town gossips, then I think you have very little to worry about."

"I just feel Mary deserved a better start than that," Joseph confessed.

"Nonsense!" Caleb scolded. "She seems healthy and happy and I am now an uncle! Uncle Caleb! I like the way that rolls off my tongue!"

"You would then allow me to finalize my betrothal to Mary?" Joseph asked, seizing his opportunity.

"Allow you?" Caleb challenged. "If you do not do so before I leave, you will need more than shepherds and angels to protect you!"

With that, the two friends embraced and Caleb left Joseph to sleep outdoors and plan his next move. He would give Mary one more day to prepare. The morning of the wedding day, Caleb would not let Mary back into her room so he could prepare the room for Joseph. Joseph would prepare the lamps they would need for the procession in the dark. Zechariah would prepare the ceremonial readings and prayers. Elisabeth would mind Yeshua for the first night. Finally, he dreamed, his betrothed would be his wife.

The day finally came. Caleb did not let Mary back in her room after the morning meal. Elisabeth knew this would be the night and early in the evening she lit extra lamps and made Mary put on her wedding garments and fitted her veil. Zechariah had already spent the day copying from memory passages from the Song of Solomon to read. Even the babies seemed to know something special was about to happen and were unusually quiet.

Nightfall came at last and Mary saw them first. A glow of lamps came down the path from the road. There was enough lamps and light to signal the approach of a dozen men, but she knew it would only be Joseph and Caleb. In her heart she was actually glad it was only them and not a group of strangers. It was the knock at the door that gave her a moment's hesitation. Would she ever hear the sound of someone at the door without her mind racing back to the evening of the angel in Nazareth? But everything had happened as prophesied over her, and though it had been a trying journey since then, no harm had come to them. Now she was to be married, and whatever came next, she would not be alone.

It was not the way weddings usually unfolded, but Zechariah

was determined to make this as special as possible under the circumstances. As he answered the knock at the door, he was ready to begin the first of his readings.

"What is that coming up from the wilderness like columns of smoke, perfumed with myrrh and frankincense, with all the fragrant powders of a merchant?" Zechariah's voice broke the tension that threatened to overwhelm Mary.

Joseph stepped through the door, dressed in a colourful robe that would have made his patriarchal namesake covetous. Unknown to anyone, Caleb had brought this robe with him from Jerusalem for just this occasion. Joseph's beard was oiled, gleaming in the lamplight and on his head was a garland of vines that looked more like thorns than flowers, but a perfect compliment to his rugged face and demeanour.

Caleb stepped in behind him, holding an array of lampstands ingeniously fitted together with twine. In his other hand he carried a box overflowing with textiles, flowers, and jewelry. This was the mattan, the gifts that the groom was bringing for his bride. He stepped forward past Joseph so the extra light from his lamps would herald Mary's appearance.

Elisabeth disappeared behind the bedroom curtains to bring Mary out, and at the same time swaddled Yeshua in her arms, ready for the opportunity to quiet him if he began to fuss.

Mary stepped out from behind the curtain into the light of the lamps and her white garments radiated like that of an angel. She wore layers of silk and lace that flowed to the floor, covering her feet. A garland of white Rose of Sharon flowers hung around her neck and tumbled to her knees. Her head was adorned with bands of jewels and red silk, her veil the sheerest of white silk with embroidery of jewels on the edges. Braided locks of her black hair graced her shoulders in contrast to the pure white of her apparel, in perfect compliment to the gleam of her eyes that danced with the lamplight through the veil.

Other than gasps of delight from Elisabeth, the little house was so silent they could hear the flickering of the lamps. Even Caleb was spellbound as he placed the box of gifts at her feet.

"Behold you are beautiful, my love." Zechariah continued, his voice cracking with emotion. "Your eyes are doves behind your veil. You have captivated my heart, my bride. You have captivated my heart with one glance of your eyes. You are altogether beautiful, my love, there is no flaw in you."

With those words spoken, Joseph broke his trance and took a few steps towards Mary, bowing as if in the presence of royalty. Right on cue, Caleb bowed all the way to his knees, and there he stayed, holding his lamps so their lowered positioned lit up Mary and Joseph's faces all the more.

Elisabeth moved to the doorway to join Zechariah. The bride and groom stood before each other in the middle of the room, their splendour on display. The brightness of Caleb's lamps appeared to make the colours of Joseph's robes reflect on Mary's radiant gown, and a holy hush settled on the room.

For minutes, the small wedding party stared in wonder at the scene before them. Joseph and Mary's eyes never left each other, as if looking away would break the spell that enveloped them. Finally, Zechariah held his parchment to the lamplight to do his next reading.

Before he could open his mouth to speak, a voice so soft and musical it was like the bubbling waters of a stream flowed from the silence.

"My beloved is beautiful and ruddy, distinguished among ten thousand. This is my beloved and this is my friend, O daughters of Jerusalem." Mary spoke so delicately that not even her veil fluttered with her speech. She had secretly looked at the parchments that Zechariah prepared and memorized them.

Elisabeth recognized the tone in her voice, the same tone that she used when she first arrived at her home those long months ago and prophesied. She gasped with joy as she realized the glorious hand of God upon Mary's life.

Caleb dared not look up. Joseph was astonished at her words and could not move, let alone speak, and only the straightening of his shoulders gave any clue that he was not frozen as a statue.

The music of Mary's voice bubbled into the lamplight again. "Let my beloved come to his garden, and eat its' choicest fruits."

That made Joseph move. He stepped towards Mary and bowed low again, this time finding her feet amidst the flowing robes, kissing her feet gently.

He was still bowed low when Zechariah read his next selection. "Awake, O north wind, and come O south wind! Blow upon my garden, and let its spices flow!"

With that invitation, both Joseph and Caleb rose to their feet, and headed for the door. Joseph stretched a beckoning hand for Mary to follow, with Caleb and his lamps to light the way into the night.

As they left the house, Zechariah read his final commentary. "Many waters cannot quench love, neither can floods drown it. If a man offered for love, all the wealth of his house, he would be utterly despised."

Caleb led them down the paths through the garden, making the walk as long as possible. Reaching the door to their room, he turned aside so they could enter. He put out the lamps one by one as he returned to the main door of the house.

Joseph stepped into the room first, and then, with both hands on Mary's arms, led her inside. The sleeping mats were already spread out, and Caleb had sprinkled them with fragrant flowers from the field. For the first time, Mary's mat was not positioned at Joseph's feet, but beside his.

They did not speak, as if not to spoil the mystery that surrounded their journey together. Neither did they undress. Joseph put out the lamp and they laid in the darkness. Joseph stroked her face, wiping tears from her eyes as he did so. Mary snuggled under his arm, happy at last to feel the strength of his touch.

Joseph was lulled to sleep by the rhythm of Mary's breathing. Mary lay awake, pondering all that had happened in the last months, and relieved that she was in the arms of her beloved at last.

Chapter Thirty-One

Trouble in Jerusalem

The next weeks passed quickly for Mary as one day blended into the next in an endless round of nursing and caring for her baby. The extended days and nights after the wedding had exhausted her, and she was glad for some days with no visitors. She was sad to see Caleb leave, as he had been her confidant in those early months of turmoil, but with Caleb gone, Joseph was more attentive to her and would often take Yeshua in the afternoon hours so she could rest.

She was surprised to find she actually enjoyed being married. Many of the women folk she grew up with often complained about their husbands and the burden that they became. Marriage was a yoke that forced them into repetitive tasks, keeping them from pursuing their own interests.

But with Joseph, she felt her yoke was easy and her burden light. He was relaxed with her. The friendly banter they had enjoyed when they were first betrothed resumed. He demanded very little of her, and anticipated her needs. She especially enjoyed their final minutes of the day together, which sometimes turned into hours.

Once Yeshua was quieted for the night, they would sit on the sleeping mats facing each other and Joseph would unravel the events of the past months, and talk of his plans for their future. Gently he would coax out her thoughts, and Mary would confide in him as she could no other. Theirs had been such a fantastic journey, sharing it with anyone else would only raise more questions without answers. Finally, they would lay down on the mats, and Mary knew she was loved and secure, whatever future stood before them.

They integrated into the slow steady rhythm of life in a small village. Mary helped Elisabeth expand the garden so they could grow more of their own food. The donkey that Joseph had purchased for their journey was traded for a pair of goats to provide milk for the growing boys.

Once the townsfolk had seen the room Joseph had built, he had enough projects to keep him as busy as he wanted to be. Many of the families could not pay him, but he took whatever they offered in vegetables or animal products. Their needs were small, and he was not trying to build a local business. They needed only to survive until it was time to move on.

They attended the local synagogue and Mary would sometimes take on sewing projects. They avoided going into Jerusalem that first year, as any contact with Jedidiah's family might raise awkward questions. Zechariah was on duty two weeks a year at the temple. On those trips he let the kinfolk know that Mary had indeed married the carpenter from Nazareth.

The boys were healthy and their antics were a pleasant distraction from the routine of life. The shaded courtyard that Joseph built alongside their room was the perfect place for the boys to spend their days. Often Joseph and Mary would create slings to carry the boys and hike into the hills that they loved.

They were content, and still very much in love. Joseph had not abandoned his dream of building his own home one day, but knew the time had not yet come. Mary felt safe and secure there. After months of anxiety at the beginning of their journey together, he would do nothing to put that kind of stress on her again.

Baby John was now two years old, and Zechariah wanted them all to go to Jerusalem for the Passover. As a priest, he was expected to go and serve at the temple at least one day during Passover week. Joseph was not so keen on the idea. He had not been able to go every year as a child, and did not see a good reason for going with the boys at so young an age.

Mary had gone every year until the death of her parents, and she missed the ceremony and pageantry of the festival. They had not travelled beyond the village since their arrival, and Mary thought a couple days away would be a welcome change.

Caleb had only visited them once, when Yeshua was about a year old. He had sold the house in Nazareth and was in Jerusalem now. Going to Jerusalem would be a chance for them to spend some time with Uncle Caleb, a moniker he demanded to be called.

Zechariah's persistence prevailed, and they prepared for the Passover journey with plans to stay at Zebediah's house. John was toddling about now, so Mary was sure his antics would be enough of a distraction to avoid any awkward questions about Yeshua.

The feast of the Passover lasted a whole week in Jerusalem. Families could celebrate the Paschal supper at the beginning of the week or at the end of the week at the Feast of Tabernacles. The days in between would be spent presenting their offerings at the temple or working as needed to prepare for the next round of sacred celebrations. Mary's family had always celebrated the Paschal at the beginning of the week and presented their offerings at the temple in the days following. They would return after that so they would not have to travel on the Sabbath.

With this scenario in mind, they prepared to go. Because they would be home by the end of Passover week, Elisabeth was determined to prepare her home before they left. Every corner of the house was swept clean, and any residue of leaven was removed. Once satisfied all was in order, she and Mary prepared the special foods for the many meals they would share. Elisabeth baked the unleavened bread while Mary harvested the bitter herbs they would need.

The day came for them to leave. The road was busy with other families from villages far away making their pilgrimage to Jerusalem. Mary could not help but remember the times she had walked this road alone and all the turmoil that had filled her heart. But now, walking with her husband, she felt her life was as normal as it would probably ever be while raising a child whose birth had been shrouded in such mystery.

Jedidiah and his household were thrilled to have them in their home for the Festival. Everyone was especially pleased to meet Joseph after all they had heard about him, doubly pleased to have a real carpenter at their disposal. As Mary hoped, John was the main attraction with his toddling and babbling. They were pleased that Joseph and Mary had been blessed with a child so quickly, but no awkward questions arose.

It was especially wonderful to be with Caleb again. Mary found ways to spend time with him alone, so little Yeshua could play with Uncle Caleb. In those times alone, Mary poured out her heart to him. She told him again of the strange prophecies of the aged Simeon and Anna. She reassured Caleb that Joseph was an attentive and loving husband, and she felt secure with him whatever the future held for them raising little Yeshua.

The Paschal was as meaningful as Mary had ever experienced. The stories of their history and the ceremony that had developed around the meal fascinated her. As the oldest son of the next generation, John was the centrepiece of the meal. Even as a toddler, he was prompted to repeat the questions the older children asked, much to the amusement of everyone.

They went to the temple the first day of the week after Sabbath had passed. The streets were as busy as ever, and Joseph confirmed to everyone that bringing the boys into such crowds was more trouble than it was worth.

Mary became more anxious as they approached the temple. The last time they were here, the encounters with the aged Simeon and Anna and her baby were unsettling. They were still trying to process all they had said, and what it could mean. During his duties at the temple, Zechariah had not seen either of them, so the assumption was that they had both passed away. Nevertheless, that did little to calm Mary's apprehension.

They were still at the outer courts when they heard the rumours. Dignitaries from lands east of Judea had arrived at Herod's palace, but they did not come to celebrate the Passover. They had come to celebrate the birth of a new king in Israel. They were staying as guests at the palace while Herod entertained their speculations.

But there had been no new king born in the palace. If there was, King Herod would have been the first to know, and to do something about it. Herod had been appointed by Rome to rule over the Jewish nation, and as long as the people remained subservient to Rome, could do pretty much as he pleased. Anxious to maintain his rule, he was rumoured to have expelled or murdered any rivals to his throne, even his own children. His cruelty was unmatched by any who came before him. It was rumoured one of his many wives tried to escape his tyranny by stowing away from Jerusalem in a funeral bier; a plot he discovered and thwarted.

Unpopular as he was, he maintained the temple and allowed religious rites to be celebrated as long as it did not interfere with his desires. The chief priests were often accused of conspiring with Herod to maintain their influence, using Herod's palace guards to do their bidding. The relationship between the palace and temple was always compromising and troubling to the common priests like Zechariah.

Now the news of a new king consumed the activities at the temple. Herod was quite sure that Rome had not appointed a new king in his place, and there was no adult rival to his throne that he knew of. But if a child had been born and the family was petitioning this child as the rightful king of Israel, that is something he had to stop at once. He knew the leaders considered him an illegitimate king, and they longed to anoint their own king as in the glory days of David and Solomon. So he had summoned the chief priests and scribes to discover if there was a new king born and where that might have happened.

That was the substance of the rumours that were now circulating throughout the temple. The dignitaries were apparently from Persia, a country that in ancient times had enslaved the Jewish people, but under present Roman rule were valued trading partners. They were not royalty, but magi: astronomers and sooth-sayers who advised the leaders of their own country on all matters political and religious. Herod would want to impress them and leave no doubt he was in charge in his own territory.

There was no way to avoid getting caught up in the discussions that swirled around them as they participated in the temple rituals that day. Some thought if there was a new king born it would be better to not let that tyrant Herod know. They feared what he would do if his rule was challenged. Others thought the possibility of a rival king would motivate Herod to placate his subjects to maintain his rule.

The chief priests were complying with Herod's demands to know where a new king might be born. They were anxious to curry his favour by not letting him be embarrassed in front of his distinguished guests. So the word was out to all the scribes and priests to search the Scriptures to discover where a king might be born. Everyone had their own opinion and were only too willing to share it with anyone who would listen.

By the time the men presented their offerings and rejoined the others in the Court of Women, even Zechariah was troubled by all the theories about a new king. They decided to leave straight for Zebediah's house, avoiding the marketplace that was so popular during feast days.

Another day in Jerusalem and it would be time for them to go home. Caleb spent every possible minute with Mary and Joseph, and would only let them have Yeshua for feeding and changing. They were glad for the attention. Let the others speculate about a new king; they had enough to deal with their little boy and all that had surrounded his young life.

The next morning, they said their farewells and finally left the bustle of the city. Mary was relieved that this time their visit to the temple had attracted no attention. She mentioned this to Joseph in private as they walked along, and he agreed. They were happy to shake the dust of Jerusalem off their feet and return to the obscurity of their quiet life in the country.

Zechariah was unusually quiet during their walk home, and they thought all the rumours at the temple were troubling him. They were almost home when Mary suggested that Joseph should get him to talk about it.

"What do you think of all the talk about a new king?" Joseph asked.

"I think they were all searching for a new king," Zechariah began cautiously, "when he was right there the whole time."

Having said this, he took Yeshua out of Joseph's arms and carried him the rest of the way home. Now it was Mary and Joseph who were troubled, as they realized what the aging priest was saying.

Chapter Thirty-Two

Magi

Joseph was awakened by the muffled voices outside. Dawn had just broken over the eastern hills, and for a moment he thought he was back at the khan, hearing the travellers stir.

But no, he was in his room with Mary beside him and Yeshua in the crib he had built. They had just returned from Passover in Jerusalem the day before and he was so exhausted he must be hearing things.

But there were the voices again. Joseph rose, careful not to disturb Mary or Yeshua, and put on his cloak. Stepping outside, he could see the source of the voices standing at the end of the stone path leading to the house.

After living with Zechariah for almost a year and a half, he recognized most of the villagers and farmers who might be on the road this early in the morning.

These were no villagers. They were dressed in tunics that reached to the ground and covered their feet. Three of them wore headpieces but each one was different. One resembled the headdress of a priest; another was like the turbans Joseph had seen travellers from Damascus wear; the third was the strangest of all, resembling a military helmet with a plume of feathers on top.

Two others were dressed in plainer attire and appeared to have dropped their packages and boxes at their feet. For whatever reason, they had stopped here for a rest and occasionally pointed to the sky as if to coax the sun from behind the last hill.

As Joseph approached to help them on their way, he noticed the men dressed in the tunics had unusual necklaces and chains hanging around their necks. On some of the chains hung ornaments the likes of which Joseph had never seen before. Even in the dim morning light, he could see the chains and pendants were made of brass and silver. The only one Joseph recognized resembled the familiar Star of David encased in a circle.

"Are you lost or just stopping for a rest?" Joseph ventured, not even sure if these strangers spoke his language.

"We were lost," the tallest one answered in Aramaic, a language Joseph spoke.

"And now we have found what we were looking for," another confirmed.

"And what would that be?" Joseph wanted to know.

"You!" they answered with laughter in their voices.

"Well, not exactly you," the tallest one explained. "But this house, and the young child who lives here."

"How do you know who lives here?" Joseph challenged them. It was no secret that children lived here, but how would they know that?

"You would be very surprised to find out all we know," the third man in a tunic answered.

"And we will be only too pleased to tell you," the tallest man suggested. "If you would be so kind to allow us to prepare a morning meal here. We have travelled through the night and wish to eat and rest. Then we will explain the reason for our visit."

Sensing that they meant him no harm, and not knowing how to refuse, Joseph agreed and led them to the yard where the outdoor oven was. The sun had now risen and he knew the boys would be waking, quickly waking everyone else.

"I must go and attend to the others in the house," Joseph excused himself.

Of all the strange encounters he had since the birth of Yeshua, this was certainly the strangest. As he entered the house, he paused to look back at his unexpected guests. The men in the tunics were reclining to rest, the other two busily unpacking boxes and preparing the meal. *Must be servants,* Joseph thought.

Yeshua was awake in his crib, so Joseph gave him to Mary to nurse. He withdrew to the main room and nervously waited for the others to join him. He tried to plan how he would explain their strange guests, but could think of nothing that would make any sense.

Once they were all at the table, Joseph attempted an explanation. "I was awakened early this morning by a group of travellers on the road," he began hesitantly. "They had walked through the night and needed a place to rest, so I told them they could use the cooking yard."

"We must offer them some food," Elizabeth exclaimed. "You never know when your guests could be angels."

"They brought their own," Joseph informed her, thinking that they had enough of angels for a lifetime. "They look like they are prepared for a long journey. They most certainly are not from Judea."

"Where did they say they were from?" Zechariah asked.

"They didn't say," Joseph explained. "But after they are rested, they will tell us who they are."

Mary listened quietly with Yeshua on her lap, but she knew

Joseph well enough to know when he was being evasive.

"Why did they stop here, precisely?" Mary forced Joseph to tell her.

Joseph hesitated, hoping to avoid answering her directly.

"Joseph?" Mary insisted.

"They said they were looking for this house and the child who lives here," Joseph replied with more of a question than an answer in his voice.

With that, Zechariah sprang from the table faster than any man his age should and headed for the door.

Elisabeth was quicker and blocked his path. "We will let them rest," she scolded him. "They are our guests and we will honour their wishes. We will know soon enough why they are here."

Reluctantly, Zechariah returned to the table, and busied himself writing on his tablet to amuse little John. Joseph took Yeshua from Mary and played with him, as much to distract himself as to entertain his son.

The next hours dragged on as the women busied themselves with household chores and the men minded the boys. No one dared to talk about their visitors. Once Mary glanced out the window to see what these travellers looked like, but they were all reclining and she could not even see how many there were.

Finally, they heard the voices of the men outside and knew that they had finished their rest. Elisabeth instructed Joseph to invite them into the house where they could explain themselves to everyone at once.

Dutifully, Joseph went outside to talk to the travellers, hoping that he had misunderstood what they had said and that they would just be on their way.

"We thank you for your hospitality," the tallest one began.

"Allow me to introduce myself."

"Actually," Joseph interrupted him, "we would like to invite you into the house to meet my family and tell us of your journey."

"That is most kind of you," another replied. "And that is precisely why we have come."

Joseph's hope that they would just be on their way was not to be. As he heard them speaking a language he did not recognize, the two men he now assumed were servants rummaged through their sacks. They gave each of the men in tunics a colourful bag to carry. As he led them to the house, only the men in tunics followed, and Joseph thought what a strange procession they made.

As they entered, Joseph saw that Elisabeth and Mary were sitting with the boys on the bench at the back of the room.

Zechariah stood and was the first to speak. "Shalom. It is an honour for you to enter my humble abode."

"Shalom indeed," the tallest one bowed as he reciprocated. "But the honour is ours. I am Balthazar. These are my companions, Melchior and Caspar," he informed them while each bowed as their name was spoken.

"I am Zechariah, a priest of the Most High God," Zechariah bowed in return, then continued, waving his arm in the direction of the women and children. "This is my wife, Elisabeth, and my son, John."

"I am Joseph," Joseph offered, taking his cue from Zechariah. "And my wife, Mary, and our son, Yeshua."

As he said Yeshua, all three of the men bowed again, only this time they bowed so low their faces almost touched the rough stone floor. *What a strange custom these foreigners have,* Joseph thought.

Elisabeth and Mary bowed their heads as their names were

spoken. Elisabeth quickly looked up, but Mary could not. Who were these men and why were they here? Their robes made them look like some kind of religious order, so she hoped they were here to visit Zechariah. Her life with Joseph had settled into a peaceful routine after all the anxiety surrounding the birth of Yeshua, and she wanted it to continue that way.

Finally, she looked up, astonished to see the men bowed low to the floor.

Melchior straightened himself and fixed his gaze on Mary. "We are magi."

Chapter Thirty-Three
The Star

"You are what?" Joseph blurted out.

"We are magi" Balthazar repeated as he rose to his feet.

Zechariah motioned for his guests to find a spot at the table. They seated themselves with their long tunics flowing around them and placed their bags on the table. Joseph saw the troubled look on Mary's face and joined her on the bench with Yeshua. Elisabeth put a fresh jug of water and clean cups on the table and returned to the bench.

"You are the magi who were in Jerusalem these past days?" Zechariah asked.

"Yes," Caspar confirmed. "Did that news reach all the way here?"

"It did, because it travelled back with us!" Zechariah exclaimed. "We were all in Jerusalem for the Passover. The temple and the whole city was in an uproar because of the news of a new king."

"That seemed strange to us," Balthazar admitted. "We went to the palace thinking that we would be the last ones to know about a new king. Apparently, we were the first to know."

"There is good reason for that," Zechariah explained. "King Herod was appointed by Rome and has never been regarded as a legitimate King of the Jews. To maintain his power he has expelled, imprisoned, or killed any rivals to his rule, even his own sons. So no one would dare to mention another king to sit on the throne of David."

"Until we showed up to make the announcement," Melchior surmised.

When Zechariah mentioned the throne of David, Mary grew increasingly anxious. How could she ever forget her angel visitor telling her the Lord God will give her son the throne of his ancestor David and his reign will have no end? Yeshua was getting restless, so she gave him to Elisabeth, who kept the boys playing on the floor in front of them.

"That explains a lot," Caspar reasoned. "Not only did no one know of any new king being born, there was this interrogation going on about where a king would be born, if not at the palace."

"What convinced you a new king had been born at all?" Zechariah inquired.

"That is a long story," Melchior cautioned, "that happened over the course of a year and more. But we will keep it as simple as possible."

"As we explained at the palace, we are magi." Balthazar began. "Melchoir and I are from Babylon, and Caspar is from Arabia. We study the stars and planets in the sky. We believe that God reveals his plans for mankind in the heavens."

"Our ancient texts declare that God set the moon and stars to rule over the night," Zechariah agreed. "Just as the sun rules over the day."

"Precisely," Caspar confirmed. "I observed that the planet we call the King planet merged very closely with the little king planet in the constellation Pisces. This is a very rare occurrence and the result of this conjunction appears as a very bright star."

"We observed the same phenomenon in Babylon," continued Balthazar. "But then an even rarer event happened. We saw the planet Mars rise between the two king planets, and interpreted this as a special sign."

"I saw the same star rising and immediately left for Babylon to discover its meaning." Caspar said.

"We consulted all the ancient texts of the Babylonians, the Medes, and the Persians," Balthazar explained. "Not until we consulted your ancient Jewish texts did we find the answer we were looking for."

Melchior continued. "The rising star happened during your Feast of Trumpets, on the exact day that you would announce the crowning of a new king of the Jews."

"So that is why you travelled to Jerusalem!" Zechariah exclaimed.

"Exactly!" Balthazar explained. "We convinced the king's court that we should travel as emissaries to bring gifts and homage to the new king. They agreed and so we have travelled for months to get to Jerusalem."

"We arranged an audience with King Herod, and gave him the gifts and messages we brought from our kingdom," Melchior continued. "When we inquired about the new king being born, he knew nothing about it. After our long journey, imagine our disappointment when no one knew of the new king!"

Joseph and Mary struggled to comprehend all that they were being told. They sat very close together and Joseph held Mary's arm as if to support her. Elisabeth minded the boys and they could not tell if she was clucking at the children, or in response to what she was hearing. Zechariah was beside himself with excitement. Even as they were talking, he retrieved his tablets and parchments and scribbled furiously.

"The palace summoned the priests from the temple to determine where the king you seek was to be born," Zechariah offered. "That was all anyone could talk about the day we were at the temple. What did they conclude?"

"It took them all day to decide that if a king in Israel was to be born, he would be born in Bethlehem," Balthazar answered.

"One of your ancient prophets Micah proclaimed that out of Bethlehem, though it is a little town out of thousands in Judah, will come a ruler of Israel."

"Of course!" Zechariah exclaimed. "I do not have a scroll of Micah, but I remember such a reference."

"Not only were they not aware a new king had been born," Melchior continued, "but after all their consultation, they obviously didn't even have the right location of the birth."

Joseph rose to his feet, and could feel Mary tugging on his cloak as if to hold him down. "Yes, they did," Joseph informed them with a steady voice. "We were only planning to be in Bethlehem for a short stop on our way here. But we did not make it in time, and Mary gave birth to our son Yeshua in Bethlehem."

"And that birth happened a year and a half ago?" calculated Balthazar.

"It is as you say," Joseph confirmed as he sat down again, glancing at Mary with that look of bewilderment he had when things were out of his control.

Mary felt bewildered herself. These astronomers were telling them that in countries a thousand miles away, the birth of her son was being proclaimed in the heavens. And now the news of the birth was being spread throughout the palace and the temple!

"So the priests were right after all!" Caspar concluded.

"Now I am confused," Zechariah admitted. "If you were told the child was born in Bethlehem, how did you know to come here?"

"Once we were told that the child was to be born in Bethlehem," Balthazar explained, "King Herod summoned us into his court for a private audience. He wanted to know all about the rising star we had seen, so we described it to him just as we have told you."

"He told us to go search for the child," Melchior continued. "And that when we found him, to return to the palace to inform him so he could celebrate as well."

"Celebrate indeed!" Zechariah mocked.

"We decided that we would leave the next morning," Caspar said. "Which would have been today. But as soon as I laid down to sleep, I had an amazing dream. It was as if God was telling me not to return to Herod once we had found the child. It was so powerful on my mind, I could not get back to sleep so I woke the others to tell them of my dream."

"We discussed what it could mean," confirmed Melchior. "And decided if we should not report back to King Herod, then maybe we should make sure he does not know where we go. So we awoke our servants and told them that we were leaving the palace immediately."

"And secretly," Balthazar added. "It was just after midnight, and we have no problem travelling at night. The stars are as good a guide at night as the sun is during the day, if you know what to look for."

"You were very wise men," Zechariah congratulated them. "Herod has his spies everywhere, so there is no doubt he would have had you followed, or had spies awaiting your arrival in Bethlehem. He built a summer palace high on a hill from which Bethlehem is in plain view. He would see your every move."

"After all the uproar at the palace, and King Herod's secretive behaviour, we had our suspicions as well," Balthazar agreed. "We managed to get outside the palace without being seen and just went through the city gate to head south to Bethlehem when we saw the star again."

"It is a phenomenon even we cannot explain," Melchior admitted. "It appeared to be the same rising star that we had seen months ago, though that would be impossible! We may spend the rest of our lives trying to figure out what it was. It was not rising to the south in the direction of Bethlehem, but westward from Jerusalem."

"We rejoiced when we saw the star again," Caspar said with excitement still in his voice. "It confirmed that we had not journeyed in vain. But it did present a dilemma. Do we follow the star where it appears to be leading us, or continue to Bethlehem where we were told to search?"

"We had to decide quickly, as we did not know how long this star, or comet, or whatever it was, would be visible," Balthazar told them. "So we decided to follow the star as that was how we began this journey. Perhaps our going to the palace was an unfortunate diversion."

"We changed our course and followed the star west out of Jerusalem," Melchior told them. "In truth, I am not sure we were following this star, or the star was following us. But when we came to the path to your house, the star seemed to maintain its position. So we stopped here to see what would happen."

"And as quickly as it appeared, the star vanished out of the sky." Balthazar told them. "And we knew we had witnessed an astronomical phenomenon."

"And we knew we had found the newborn King of the Jews," Melchior concluded triumphantly. "That is when Joseph approached us, and why we told him we were lost, but now had found what we were looking for."

No one knew what to say. It was a fantastic tale of dreams and stars, intrigue and premonitions. And if what they said was true, then little Yeshua playing on the floor at their feet was destined to become a king.

Elisabeth rocked John to sleep and cooed softly. Zechariah furiously scribbled on his tablets and parchments. Joseph scooped up Yeshua and paced the floor, realizing that child was destined for a future far beyond what a poor carpenter could prepare him for.

Mary stared blankly with a dozen voices swirling through her head.

"He will be great and will be called Son of the Most High."

"Who am I, that the mother of my Lord should visit me?"

"Mary, you think too much."

"The Lord God will give him the throne of his ancestor David."

"Behold, a virgin shall conceive."

"And so the child will be holy and will be called Son of God."

"For unto us is born this day, in the city of David, a Saviour."

"We had found the newborn King of the Jews."

"Mary, you think too much."

"I am the handmaid of the Lord. Let what you have said be done to me."

"Yes, a sword shall pierce through your own soul also."

Mary could feel that sword now. *How could she be the mother to a king, perhaps even a son of the Most High? And what about Joseph? Is this what he signed up for when he married her?*

Joseph sat down again beside her, and she buried her head

between his shoulder and Yeshua's face. The tears she could not hold back any longer flowed freely as Joseph stroked her hair.

Chapter Thirty-Four
The Gift

Yeshua began to fuss so Mary took him from Joseph, cradling him on her lap. Elisabeth took John to his sleeping mat and returned to sit on the bench where Zechariah joined her.

What a story they had just heard! Everything the magi said confirmed what they had experienced over the last two years. Yeshua was destined to be a king, but how that would come about and what kind of kingdom that would look like no one could imagine.

The awkward silence was finally broken by Zechariah. "Our ancient texts tell us that this king, this Messiah, will be a light to the Gentiles, and to the whole world," he announced. "And so it is fitting that a light should bring you to him."

"We are magi," Balthazar informed them. "We may walk in darkness, but we have seen a great light."

"And that light has led us here," Melchior concluded.

"That is why we do not regard him as just the King of the Jews," Caspar said as he reached for one of the bags on the table. "But our king as well."

With that said, Caspar took his bundle and rose from the table. He walked towards Mary and Yeshua, never fully straightening up. Once he was close to the bench, he settled on his knees and bowed low, placing his bag in front of him.

Distracted by the spectacle before him, Yeshua quieted in Mary's arms. Mary wished she could quiet the voices swirling in her head as easily as she could quiet Yeshua. Joseph rose from the bench and settled on his knees as well. He had no idea how he should respond, but if magi could travel a thousand miles to pay their respects, he could do no less.

What a sight they made! The aging Arabian magi in his brightly coloured robe and turban, and the rugged young Galilean carpenter framed by a simple Judean farmhouse! Both on their knees in front of a young mother and her little child.

Balthazar and Melchior joined them on their knees in front of Mary and Yeshua. They also bowed low and placed their bundles at the feet of Mary. Mary looked at Elisabeth, searching her face for direction on how she was to respond, but Elisabeth was no help. Her face beamed with the same joy she had greeted Mary with those many months ago.

Caspar untied the strap that fastened his bag. Out of it he removed a small brightly coloured jug. He pulled the wooden plug out of the jug and poured a tiny amount of the liquid on the cloth.

"This is myrrh," he began. "It is a perfume from my country that is highly valued and used in every type of ceremony from birth to death. Its most important usage is to anoint our kings."

Caspar dipped his finger in the little pool of myrrh on the cloth and touched it to the forehead of little Yeshua. Yeshua reached for the man's hand as it neared his face, and for a brief moment the child from Bethlehem held the hand of the Arabian. Mary did nothing to prevent this from happening. Lost in her thoughts, she was more of a spectator than a participant in the scene unfolding before her.

Melchior untied his bag next to reveal a taller, slender bottle.

"Frankincense is a precious oil we burn as incense," he explained. "Priests of every nation burn frankincense in their temples of worship."

As if they had rehearsed, Zechariah left the bench to retrieve the small clay dish he used for incense and offered it to Melchior. He poured a few drops into the dish and Zechariah returned it to the table and proceeded to light it. Joseph watched in wonder as the little house indeed became a temple, with a priest and worshippers and this little child that he was told would save people from their sins.

"We have travelled long and far to meet this child," Balthazar began. "And we know that your journey will be long and far as well. So we bring gold for his treasury to sustain him on his journey until he takes his rightful throne."

Mary could scarcely believe what she heard. The angel visitor had told her that her child would take the throne of his ancestor David. Now these magi had travelled for months to confirm what she was told. It was all too amazing to comprehend.

Balthazar untied his parcel and removed a leather purse. He opened the mouth of the purse and took out a handful of gold coins, letting them slip through his fingers to the floor. The tinkling and shine of the metal drew the attention of Yeshua and he almost squirmed out of Mary's arms to reach for them, babbling as he did so.

The magi smiled at his antics and Elisabeth had to stifle her laughter. It was enough to break the solemnity of the moment. Laughing now themselves, the magi rose to their feet, leaving their treasures at the feet of Mary and Yeshua. Joseph rose to his feet as well, and not knowing how to thank the magi, he bowed to them.

"It is now well past the ninth hour," Zechariah informed them all. "You must stay and share our evening meal with us."

"That is most kind," Balthazar answered, "but we must be on our way. We have been warned about King Herod, so we must leave his territory as quickly as possible."

"Tomorrow will be your Sabbath," Melchior reminded them. "It is best we are out of Judean territory by then."

Zechariah realized the wisdom of their haste and agreed that they should go. The magi left the house to inform their servants it was time to prepare to leave. Joseph told the others that he would join the magi for a short while, as a grateful host.

The magi bid their farewell and blessing upon the child king and they walked down the stone path and followed the road west into Ain Karim. Mary watched the travellers until they were out of sight, and then retired to her room with Yeshua; exhilarated and exhausted.

Joseph was not usually an avid talker, especially with strangers, but this day was different. As they walked along, he told the magi their own story of his betrothal to Mary, all the turmoil of her being with child, and the events that happened in Bethlehem and Jerusalem.

The magi questioned him throughout, amazed at Joseph's story. They encouraged him by saying with all that had happened so far, he did not need to fear what lay ahead. Finally, Joseph had gone far enough, and with final farewells, headed back home. As he returned, he wished he had talked less and let them tell him about the stars in the heavens. Nevertheless, he was glad he had walked with them, and thought what an incredible day it had been since he was first awakened by these mysterious magi.

It was almost dark as he arrived home. Before he entered the house, he paused to gaze at the first stars of the evening. He knew nothing about the skies or constellations or astronomy, but as he looked upward, he wondered if the light in the night sky that the magi saw happened on the night Yeshua was born. What if that light was the blinding light of the angels that the shepherd boys had told him about? Could the light of a heavenly host be seen a thousand miles away? He did not know, but was learning that with the Most High, anything was possible.

Zechariah and Elisabeth were already in their room with John for the night. The remnants of the evening meal still lay on the table, but Joseph did not need to eat. His appetite was satiated by a heart full of courage for the task before him. He was now more determined than ever to raise this child in the fear of the Lord. If his destiny was to be king, and save his people from their sins, he would learn what that meant when the time came.

After Joseph left with the magi, Mary had rested with Yeshua on her mat. At Elisabeth's insistence, she had sat at the evening meal, but even the boys ate more than she did. She nursed Yeshua and put him to sleep, and then lay on her mat, lost in her thoughts as she waited for Joseph to return.

When Joseph lay down beside her at last, she began to relax. He told her how he told their story to the magi, and how they had encouraged him. He told her of his new resolve to raise this child to be a king, or a saviour, or whatever the Lord willed.

Mary finally opened her heart and told of all she had thought throughout the day. She realized that all the angel had told her had come true. The truth of the birth of Yeshua had been confirmed by Elisabeth, shepherds, angels, and the aging Simeon and Anna at the temple. And now, years later, they learn that foreigners from a thousand miles away had been told of the birth and destiny of her child.

"Joseph?" Mary prodded. "Those were strange gifts to give a child, don't you think? What are we to do with them?"

"I'm not sure what we are to do," he admitted. "But if you think the child is a king, then maybe they are exactly right. Besides, they have given us a gift far greater."

"What gift is that?" Mary wanted to know.

"The gift of knowing God is with us," Joseph replied thoughtfully. "If God would use the stars in the heavens to guide these foreigners to worship this child of the Most High, then surely He will guide us. You no longer have to ponder about all that has happened surrounding the birth of Yeshua. Everything the angel told you, and told me, was true. We have been living here, not sure what it all meant and what we are to do. We should stop wondering now and start planning how to raise this child."

Mary agreed, snuggling into Joseph's arms. She loved this man that God had given her to help raise her child of promise. Many nights in the past they laid awake wondering and worrying. Tonight, they held each other close and quickly fell into a dreamless sleep.

Made in the USA
Monee, IL
04 November 2021